# A FOOL I' THE FOREST

# A Fool i' the Forest

## A PHANTASMAGORIA

RICHARD ALDINGTON

*with an introduction and notes by*

MICHAEL COPP

ELIZABETH VANDIVER

RENARD PRESS

**RENARD PRESS LTD**

124 City Road
London EC1V 2NX
United Kingdom
info@renardpress.com
020 8050 2928

www.renardpress.com

*A Fool i' the Forest* first published in 1925
This edition first published by Renard Press Ltd in 2025

*A Fool i' the Forest* © the Estate of Richard Aldington
Introduction and Notes © Michael Copp and Elizabeth Vandiver, 2025

Cover design by Will Dady

Printed on FSC-accredited papers in the UK by 4edge Limited

ISBN: 978-1-80447-171-5

9 8 7 6 5 4 3 2 1

EU Authorised Representative: Easy Access System Europe
Mustamäe tee 50, 10621 Tallinn, Estonia
gpsr.requests@easproject.com.

# CONTENTS

# NOTE

The application of this phantasmagoria will be apparent when the symbolical nature of the three characters – 'I', Mezzetin, the Conjuror – is explained.

The trio are one person split into three.

'I' is intended to be typical of a man of our own time, one who is by temperament more fitted for an art than a scientific civilisation. He is shown at a moment of crisis, and the phantasmagoria is the mirror of his mind's turmoil as he struggles to attain a harmony between himself and the exterior world.

Mezzetin comes from the Commedia dell'Arte. He symbolises here the imaginative faculties – art, youth, satire, irresponsible gaiety, liberty. He is one or several of these by turns and all together.

In a similar manner the Conjuror symbolises the intellectual faculties – age, science, righteous cant, solemnity, authority – which is why I make him so malicious.

Several quotations are woven into the piece; the two longest are from Aristophanes and Anatole France.

RICHARD ALDINGTON

# INTRODUCTION

The long poem *A Fool i' the Forest* is Richard Aldington's most sustained poetic expression of his ongoing struggles with overcoming the trauma of his military service in the First World War. This complex poem, 1343 lines in thirty-four numbered sections, is written in an allusive, fragmentary, quotation-laden style reminiscent of *The Waste Land*, to which it is frequently compared (see below), although Aldington himself denied any connection between the two works.[1] *Fool* traces the internal conflicts and eventual dissolution of a personality in the decade following the war. It grapples with the aftermath of war both personal and societal, the development of trends in modern poetry, and the overall direction of society in the mid-1920s. In the poem, three aspects of one character – called 'I', Mezzetin and the Conjuror – struggle, and ultimately fail, to find some way of reconciling their differences and living with one another.

---

1 For a detailed comparison of *Fool* and *The Waste Land*, see Oliver Tearle's *The Great War, The Waste Land and the Modernist Long Poem*, pp. 135–43.

# Richard Aldington: Biography and Context[2]

Born in 1892, Richard Aldington grew up in and around Dover. His childhood years were largely unhappy and his family dysfunctional. His father Albert Aldington was an ineffective solicitor whose unwise financial investments led to two episodes of bankruptcy, while his mother May was a much stronger character who came to despise her husband. Aldington includes scathing portraits of his parents in his novels *Death of a Hero* (1929) and *Very Heaven* (1937). While savage, these portrayals are probably not entirely unjustified. Albert Aldington's financial difficulties meant Richard was removed from Dover College, which he attended as a day boy, at the age of thirteen and, later, had to leave University College London at the age of eighteen after only one year's attendance as an undergraduate. Aldington was therefore largely self-educated in languages, literature and history, a fact that he often disguised by implying that he had received a typical public-school and university education.

His parents' unhappy marriage probably contributed to Aldington's own psychological vulnerability, and in particular to his inability to form a lasting marital attachment. His marital problems, in turn, exacerbated his depression and sense of alienation during his military service in the First World War and in the decade that followed. Before the war, Aldington had thrived in the all-too-brief period when

---

2 For details of Aldington's biography, see Vivien Whelpton, *Richard Aldington: Poet, Soldier and Lover. 1911–1929*. We are grateful to her for her assistance with this introduction.

he began to publish his poetry, co-founded the Imagist movement, became part of a literary circle in which he could flourish, met his companion and later wife, the American poet Hilda Doolittle (H.D.), whom he admired and deeply loved, and served as assistant editor of the journal *The Egoist*. War disrupted all of this, even Aldington's and H.D.'s marriage, and the marriage was also damaged by the birth of a still-born daughter in May 1915, an intensely traumatic experience for them both. Their physical and emotional relationship deteriorated over the next year, and by 1916, when it became obvious that married men would be conscripted, Aldington sought solace in a brief extra-marital affair. By March 1918, with his second period of service at the front looming, he was immersed in a far more passionate and emotionally serious affair with Dorothy Yorke, and H.D. left London to join the composer Cecil Gray in Cornwall. When she became pregnant by Gray, Aldington agonised over whether he would be capable of treating her child as his own. He was especially distressed at the notion of this child replacing the one he and H.D. had lost. The letters he wrote to H.D. in this period reflect his tormented emotions over their situation.[3] He vacillated between pleading with H.D. to continue their marriage and promising to care for her and her child, and declaring that he could not possibly love her baby as though it were his own and that therefore they must break with one another. At the same time, he was also torn between his abiding love for H.D. and his passion for his lover, Dorothy Yorke. H.D.'s daughter was born on the 31st

---

3 Caroline Zilboorg's *Richard Aldington & H.D.: Their Lives in Letters, 1918–1961* prints Aldington's letters to H.D. from this period. Unfortunately, H.D.'s letters to Aldington from the war era have not survived.

of March 1919, and the couple separated a few weeks later. Aldington would spend the next nine years living with Yorke in the Berkshire countryside.

His war experiences are vividly recreated in *Death of a Hero*, and in his collection of short stories, *Roads to Glory* (1930). He enlisted in May 1916 and arrived at the Loos sector of the Western Front in January 1917. His battalion, the 11th Leicesters, were the Pioneers of 6th Division – units assigned to construct trenches, roads and railways, but also to serve as infantry when so required. The surroundings were unrelievedly grim, work as a pioneer was taxing, and the rear areas where Aldington was billeted were under constant shellfire and intermittent gas bombardments. He undertook officer training in England, starting in May 1917, and did not return to the front until nearly a year later, in the aftermath of the 1918 German Spring Offensive; by then he was commissioned as a second-lieutenant in the 9th Battalion of the Royal Sussex Regiment. He soon became an acting company commander. In late August 1918 he began a six-week signals course, and rejoined his battalion as its signals officer on the 8th of October. He took part in the final battle of the Hindenburg Line, the Battle of Cambrai, and participated on the 4th of November in the advance across the River Rhonelle.

Aldington's military service did not end with the Armistice of the 11th of November, as the 9th Sussex became part of the Army of Occupation and he was not demobilised until February 1919. War-weary and in poor health, attempting to deal at a distance with the conflict he was experiencing between his love for H.D. and his passion for Yorke as well as with the emotional impact of H.D.'s pregnancy, having no employment to which to return and devoid of creative inspiration,

Aldington sank into a depressed state. After demobilisation, he returned to London and found lodging in a shabby hotel. He tried to support himself by writing journal articles; his one stroke of good fortune was his appointment as French critic for the *Times Literary Supplement*. The final rupture with H.D. in April was abrupt and acrimonious, although the exact details remain obscure. H.D. later wrote that Aldington's emotional state at the time had verged on insanity.

In December 1919 he left London for the Berkshire countryside, where Yorke joined him a year later and where he adopted a punishing routine of reading, translating (primarily French texts) and reviewing.[4] The *TLS* earned him a living, but he still needed to place articles elsewhere, for the purposes of both income and reputation; *TLS* reviews were anonymous. Despite his heavy workload, residing in the Berkshire countryside seems to have given him some peace, although he was still unable to put his war memories entirely behind him; he was clearly suffering from what would later be called Post-Traumatic Stress Disorder. *Exile and Other Poems* (1923) was Aldington's first substantial attempt to process the trauma of his experience in poetry, to that point his dominant creative form.

His view of the state of the nation and its culture was profoundly gloomy, and he was sceptical of the directions contemporary poetry seemed to be taking, seeing it as either ordered but effete or vigorous but shapeless. He found himself on the horns of a dilemma, wanting in his writing to reject the increasing intellectual elitism of Pound or Eliot, but out of tune both with wider society and with current literary trends.

---

4 Aldington first lived in the hamlet of Hermitage but moved to the village of Padworth in December 1920.

Nevertheless, he clung to a belief in the life of the senses, and also to a faith in humanity which contrasts sharply with the pessimism of much of his writing of the time.

In early February 1924, he began work on *A Fool i' the Forest*, a departure from anything he had ever attempted before. His introductory Note to the poem described it as a depiction of 'a man of our own time... shown at a moment of crisis... as he struggles to attain a harmony between himself and the exterior world.'[5] He was working simultaneously on a monograph on Voltaire, for which he undertook a massive amount of reading. The combination of his demanding routine and the emotional toll taken by writing *A Fool i' the Forest* led to a result that was perhaps inevitable: in February 1925 he collapsed from nervous exhaustion.

## *The Long Modernist Poem*

Aldington was far from alone in turning to the long narrative poem as a means of expressing the dislocation and alienation of the 1920s. The decade is noteworthy for a flood of modernist works of literature, both in poetry and in fiction. 1922 was dominated by the publication of T.S. Eliot's *Waste Land* and James Joyce's *Ulysses*. Three years later, in 1925, there was a second important wave: Virginia Woolf's novel, *Mrs Dalloway*, and two long modernist poems: Nancy Cunard's *Parallax* and Aldington's *A Fool i' the Forest*. Strictly speaking, the decade begins with Hope Mirrlees's *Paris: A Poem*, published in 1919. All these long poems

---

5 For the introductory Note, see p. 7.

constitute an inter-related group and interact with one another. The later ones inevitably echo, reflect and differ from, or converge with each other's prosody and structure, as well as with each other's themes: personal despair, the war, criticism of contemporary society, the metropolis, myth, literary allusion and colonialism.

It was perhaps inevitable that any long Modernist poem appearing in 1925, as both Aldington's *Fool* and Nancy Cunard's *Parallax* did, should be initially dismissed as an imitation of *The Waste Land*. But Aldington and Cunard were not copyists or plagiarists; their poems are better read as responses to, allusions to and commentaries on Eliot's work. *The Waste Land* differs in several key ways from these other poems. Most obviously, *Fool* and *Parallax*, like Mirrlees's *Paris*, are basically structured as narratives and employ the figure of a guide or narrator in the form of a flâneur or flâneuse who makes his or her way through a phantasmagoria. In contrast, *The Waste Land* consists of a loose sequence of themes, images and events, whose interconnectedness is not immediately apparent. It has no consistent narrator; several passages are in the first-person singular, but these are in different narrative voices.

In *Fool*, the primary guide/narrator, identified as 'I', contrasts the ancient civilisation of Greece, which he conceives of as emphasising simplicity, harmony, order and beauty, with the modern civilisation of post-war Britain: inharmonious, hypocritical, mechanical and corrupted by commerce and materialism. People lead dead, empty lives, and poetry has been degraded as well: 'Our poets are all journalists, clerks and schoolmasters' (Section IX). The narrator's thoughts and conclusions are constantly

15

questioned and challenged by his two companions: the Conjuror and the fool Mezzetin.[6] Both are closely implicated in the narrator's striving towards some sort of resolution of his personality and of the many problems that beset him. This tripling of his persona makes Aldington's poem very different not only from *The Waste Land* but from other long Modernist poems as well, as it foregrounds the question of whether the narrator 'I' will be able to achieve some sort of equilibrium by means of a synthesis of the intellectual, solemn, authoritative side (the Conjuror), with the artistic, imaginative, irresponsible side (Mezzetin).

Aldington consistently denied that *Fool* was influenced by Eliot. In a 1927 letter to Herbert Read he said that the structure of *Fool* was drawn not from *The Waste Land*, but from May Sinclair's long poem *The Dark Night* (1924). He added that *Fool's* sometimes whimsical tone was influenced by Osbert and Sacheverell Sitwell, and that many of the themes of *Fool* were laid out already in his 1923 collection *Exile and Other Poems*.[7] Aldington's claim that the form of *Fool* was based on May Sinclair's poem is puzzling. *The Dark Night* is a long poem in free verse, with a first-person narrator named Elizabeth. It focuses almost entirely on Elizabeth's tempestuous relationship with a poet, Victor, tracing their meeting, his early rejection of her, their marriage, his

---

6 *Parallax* and *Fool* were coterminous works as regards composition and publication, so Aldington and Cunard could not have had any knowledge of the other's work. It is, however, interesting to note that Cunard describes her wanderer through the streets of London, then in France and Italy, and, finally, back to London, as 'This clouded fool, / This poet-fool' (Nancy Cunard, *Parallax*, p. 5).

7 Richard Aldington, letter dated 'King Charles the Martyr's Day' (i.e. the 30th of January 1927) in 'Letters to Herbert Read', p. 28.

infidelity with her foster-daughter Monica, their parting and his return to her again when Monica leaves him after he becomes blind. It is divided into thirty-three sections of irregular length; in that regard, as in its use of free verse, *Fool* (with its thirty-four sections) does resemble Sinclair's poem. But although many of Aldington's other works concentrate on the relationship between the sexes and the emotional damage caused by societal strictures on sexuality (see, for example, *The Crystal World, A Dream in the Luxembourg, Death of a Hero*), in *Fool* these topics are strikingly absent. The narrator of *Fool* does marry in the end, as part of his sinking into bourgeois mediocrity, but his marriage is never presented as involving any passion, intense suffering or conflict. Moreover, in *The Dark Night* the narrative proceeds chronologically and logically, while *Fool* jumps from place to place and from time to time. In short, there is no obvious similarity between Sinclair's poem and *Fool* beyond the use of free verse and the division into sections of irregular length.[8]

---

8 The presentation of a male poet whose creative impulse leads him to waver between two women and ultimately to reject the wife on whose devotion he has depended does, of course, have obvious resonances with Aldington's own personal situation in 1918–19, when he was torn between H.D. and Dorothy Yorke. One disturbing connection which must be merely coincidental is between the situation in the poem, where Victor leaves Elizabeth because he has fallen in love with her foster-daughter Monica, and Aldington's actions in 1937, when he left his long-time companion Brigit Patmore for her daughter-in-law Netta Patmore. Interestingly, Sinclair's poem contains the line 'His soul is a crystal world, hard and clear' (Sinclair, 1924, p. 16), describing someone with whom the narrator feels a particular closeness. It seems possible that Aldington recalled this line, consciously or unconsciously, when choosing a title for his 1937 love-poem, *The Crystal World*.

# A Fool i' the Forest *and* The Waste Land

The similarities that many critics have seen to *The Waste Land* are much easier to understand, despite Aldington's denial of any influence of Eliot's poem on *Fool*. Aldington and Eliot had a long and very complicated relationship. The two men met in the summer of 1917, when Eliot took over as assistant editor of *The Egoist* from H.D. (who herself had replaced Aldington after his enlistment). At times they were close friends; in 1922 Aldington tried to raise money to allow Eliot to leave Lloyds Bank when his health seemed to depend on it, and Eliot visited Aldington as a house guest at his Berkshire cottage in the mid-1920s. But while Aldington greatly admired Eliot as a literary critic, he was ambivalent about the value of Eliot's poetry, and it is hard to determine his precise view of *The Waste Land*.

In 1941, Aldington said that Eliot's 'greatest service to English literature at that time [i.e. after the war] was his insistence that writers could not afford to throw over the European tradition'.[9] But in 1940 he had delivered a lecture on 'Ezra Pound and T.S. Eliot' at Columbia University, which was merciless to both poets' weak points; this was published in 1954. It is a witty and acerbic piece, in which Aldington objects to *The Waste Land* primarily because of its overall air of pessimistic despair and its disgusted portrayal of sexuality. Interestingly, Aldington also faults Eliot for the overuse of unacknowledged quotations, a technique that Aldington himself employed extensively in *Fool* (see below).[10] All of this

9  Richard Aldington, *Life for Life's Sake: A Book of Reminiscences*, p. 218.
10  Richard Aldington, *Ezra Pound and T.S. Eliot: A Lecture*, p. 16.

suggests that Aldington's view of *The Waste Land* was very likely already deeply ambivalent in 1924 when he was writing *Fool*.

Nevertheless, whatever Aldington himself thought about Eliot's poem, several contemporary reviewers saw strong links between *The Waste Land* and *A Fool i' the Forest*. For instance, Humbert Wolfe wrote that *Fool* 'was plainly derived from *Waste-Land* [sic]… Aldington, as a matter of fact, could only see life darkly in T.S. Eliot's looking-glass.'[11] And there are certainly some striking similarities. Aldington and Eliot are both disenchanted with London, which they perceive as embodying all the faults of a modern metropolis. They stress the sordid surroundings and collapsed values of the post-war years. To illustrate the decline of western culture, Aldington and Eliot both include musical references, taken from popular music. Eliot's Section II, 'A Game of Chess', quotes and adapts 'That Shakespearean Rag' (1912, words by Gene Buck and Herman Ruby and music by David Stamper); similarly, in Section XXV of *Fool*, Aldington adapts a rag-time song 'Are You from Dixie' (1915, words by Jack Yellen and music by George L. Cobb):

And then that Heavenly rag-time:
> *'Are you from Dixie?*
> *Yes, I'm from Dixie!*
> *Well, I'm from Dixie too-oo-oo!'*

---

11 Humbert Wolfe, *Dialogues and Monologues*, pp. 199–200. See also Paul Rosenfeld, *By Way of Art: Criticisms of Music, Literature, Painting, Sculpture, and the Dance*, pp. 240–47, Glenn Hughes, *Imagism and the Imagists: A Study in Modern Poetry*, pp. 100–06 and Norman T. Gates (ed.), *The Poetry of Richard Aldington: A Critical Evaluation and An Anthology of Uncollected Poems*, pp. 84–85.

Gorgeous, isn't it?
Such a change from Beethoven and Sousa.
And the joy of dancing it with a pure, bright girl –
    *There's a hole in her stocking...*

These last words have been slightly adapted by Aldington from the song 'Dance with a Dolly with a Hole in Her Stocking', another trite ditty. These adaptations of rag-time songs, while forming a connection between *The Waste Land* and *Fool*, also epitomise characteristic differences in Aldington's and Eliot's writing. Aldington tends to make his points with direct, unambiguous clarity, even to labour them, whereas Eliot is indirect, more discreetly allusive, less overtly obvious.

Both Eliot and Aldington include a range of foreign-language references in their respective works: discrete fragments, short phrases and partial quotations from Greek, German, French, Italian and Sanskrit. Some of Aldington's are his own creations, including the long French passage that constitutes Section XVIII. Both poets include words and precepts from the languages of eastern religions: Eliot with the Sanskrit 'Datta' (Give), 'Dayadhvam' (Sympathise), 'Damyata' (Control) and 'Shanti' (Peace); Aldington with the Hebrew 'Shemah Israel' ('Hear, O Israel'). Both their poems end with a repeated word: Eliot repeats 'Shanti' three times, and Aldington repeats the word 'Farewell' four times. A crucial difference in the two poets' use of incorporated sections in foreign languages is that Eliot provided notes for *The Waste Land*, in which he often identified the sources of quotations (although he did not give translations) and offered guidance to the reader. Aldington, strikingly, did none of this. *Fool* contains a great many embedded and adapted quotations (which we have identified, so far as we were able, in the notes to this edition), ranging from references to popular songs, to partial quotations from Shakespeare – most notably, of course, in the title – and later European poets, to direct translations and looser paraphrases of classical texts, along with indirect allusions to all of these.[12] But Aldington neither identifies nor comments on these quotations, allusions and references. Ironically, the allusive Eliot provides at least a partial key to his work's obscurities, while Aldington, despite the apparent directness of his presentation, gives the reader no such aid. This edition hopes to fill that gap.[13]

## *Aldington and Classics*

For Aldington, the classical world was far more than a storehouse of quotations or even characters (such as Eliot's Philomel and Tiresias). *Fool* is permeated with classical references, which do not only appear in quotations but are also interwoven into key elements of the narrative itself. Throughout the poem, the classical references express a sense of profound loss and longing for a tradition that is no longer truly accessible to the characters of the poem.[14]

---

12 Aldington says in the introduction to his *Complete Poems* that he used 'the device of the unacknowledged quotation' from 1912 onwards, and that the most frequent instances were in *Fool* 'and range from Sappho to Renan' (*The Complete Poems*, p. 16).

13 The only previous attempt to annotate *A Fool i' the Forest* is Robin Ancrum's *A Fool i' the Forest: A Critical Edition* M.A. thesis. This is useful but limited, omitting many important identifications, and as an MA thesis is not readily available.

14 On Aldington and classics, see Elizabeth Vandiver, *Richard Aldington's Modernist Antiquity: Classics, Imagism, and the Great War*.

Many of the titles of the poem's thirty-four sections evoke classics and the classical world, e.g. Section IV: 'Acropolis – Lament for Lord Byron'; Section IX: 'Greek Art – the Conflict and Reflections'; Section XVII: 'The Manifestation of Pallas'; Section XXI: 'Greek Science – Pagan Sensuality'. The poem's longest segment (Sections III to XXI) deals with the three characters' journey to Athens, where they visit the Acropolis, and foregrounds their sustained and at times acrimonious discussions of classical literature and culture, its importance for the modern world and its intrinsic value (or lack thereof). Throughout, Aldington assumes in his reader a wide knowledge of classical history, culture, religion and literature, often making a crucial point simply through mentioning the names of ancient writers (e.g. 'Demosthenes fades to Chrysostom', line 393). He uses the same technique with references to later literature and history, but the classical allusions in *Fool* far outnumber the allusions to any other period or culture.

## *Narrative Structure*

*Fool* is primarily narrated by 'I', who first appears in line five. In the first two sections of the poem, 'I' describes his longing for a 'Fool'. Section III introduces Mezzetin and the Conjuror (although with no explanation of who they are). The narrative then follows the three characters through their journey to Greece; their further adventures in a ruined church and on the Western Front; the return of the Conjuror and 'I' to London after Mezzetin's death; and the final vignette of 'I' as a married commuter with an office job. Although the three characters 'I', the Conjuror and Mezzetin move through different places and even different times – the poem is set in the post-war period and the Athens they visit is modern, but the characters find themselves in what appears to be a medieval church in Section XXII, and then on the Western Front during the war in Sections XXIII–XXVII – each episode proceeds chronologically and when 'I' reminisces about earlier periods in his life (as he does in Section XXIV), it is clear that he is remembering past events.

As the main narrator, 'I' includes long quotations of remarks by the Conjuror and Mezzetin. These are usually clearly identified. The narrative structure is complicated at times by the inclusion of several italicised segments, some of them also inset, which vary from single lines to the thirty-eight lines (in French) of Section XVIII. Many of these passages appear to be parodies of actual poems or songs, or at least of poetic styles. These italicised passages often seem to be 'outside' the narrative structure, not directly attributable to any of the three main characters, but there are some instances where an italicised section is attributed to a specific speaker. Most importantly, in Section XX 'I' prays to Athena with an italicised, inset prayer that is a translation from Aristophanes (see note on lines 654–64); there, the prayer is enclosed in quotation marks and is introduced by the words 'I prayed'. In Section IV, a four-line quotation is introduced by the words 'the Conjuror... spouted French', and in Section VIII, the three italicised stanzas beginning 'O, we came up to Camden Town' are apparently spoken (or sung) by Mezzetin, since they are followed by the line 'But there the Conjuror cut him short'. But other italicised passages, some quite lengthy and important to the narrative, are not set in quotation marks, nor are they attributed to any of the characters. The most important of these is 'The Culture Hymn' of Section XVI. This follows closely on and is written in the same style as 'The Yankee Orator', which 'I' attributes to Mezzetin; but 'The Yankee Orator' is printed in roman type, and is closed with a quotation mark. 'The Culture Hymn' that immediately follows, in contrast, is italicised, inset, and with no quotation marks and no attribution to any speaker. Since 'The Culture Hymn' results in an actual epiphany of the goddess Athena, it is one of the central passages of the poem, but who speaks it is left ambiguous.

## *Form and Style*

The poem is primarily written in free verse, but Aldington incorporates traditional metres throughout for effect, and displays great skill in using these. This is most noticeable in Section VI: 'The Voyage of Telemachus', which effectively echoes the dactylic hexameters of ancient epic. But Aldington also uses iambic and trochaic metres at key sections in the work. The first line of the poem, 'Court jester to an age that lacks a king', is perfect iambic pentameter, and the third and fourth lines are as well, although with feminine endings ('Some fool who thought the crowd should praise his verses / Instead of punting mildly at the races?'). Iambic pentameter lines reappear frequently throughout the poem.

Trochaic metre, in both tetrameter and pentameter lines, appears most effectively in the 'Gulf of Naples' passage of Section XXIV, where 'I' is reminiscing about his youth and framing his memories largely in terms drawn from classical literature and culture and the use of traditional metrical patterns heightens the sense of a longing for a lost tradition. Section XXXIII, too, is heavily trochaic, with occasional free-verse lines in the section describing 'I's' suburban life; line 1301, the single word 'Yet', introduces a long passage primarily in regular trochaic metre, mainly tetrameter with a few catalectic lines:

**Some**times **when** my **stal**wart **fi**gure      [tetrameter]
**Strides** the **bleak** sub**urb**an **golf**-links;      [tetrameter]
**Some**times **when** I **lie** a**wake**      [tetrameter catalectic]
(**Too** much **cof**fee **af**ter **din**ner)…      [tetrameter]
                                             (*lines 1302–05*)

This strongly trochaic pattern continues through the final lines of the section, which are in trochaic pentameter: '**Of** a **life** once **vowed** to **truth** and **beau**ty, / **Pierce** me **till** I **start** and **gasp** in **ang**uish' (lines 1321–22). In this section, too, the shift to traditional metre reflects the imagined but now lost antiquity for which the poetic side of 'I', supported by Mezzetin, deeply longed. The poem's form thus supports and underlines its presentation of the conflict in 'I's' psyche between his love for the past and the demands of the present.

## *Coda: Answers for a Murdered Self*

Aldington's post-war poetry repeatedly expresses the sense that his innermost self did not, in some fundamental sense, survive the war. His poem 'Eumenides' casts this dead self as in fact the Eumenides, the spirits of vengeance: 'It is my own murdered self… / Violently slain, which rises up like a ghost / To torment my nights… / It is myself that is the Eumenides, / That will not be appeased, about my bed'. The poem ends with the question, 'Tell me, what answer can I give my murdered self?' (*Exile*, p. 31). *Fool* also deals with a murdered self, or with two murdered parts of a tripartite self, since by the end of the poem both the poetic, creative Mezzetin and the intellectual, rational Conjuror have been killed (and the term the narrator uses is 'murdered'), and 'I' has dwindled into a suburban commuter who is only occasionally haunted by the memory of a 'ghostly mandoline' as he dutifully makes his way into London each working day.

For Aldington, as for Eliot, London embodies all the faults of the modern world and serves as a symbol of disenchantment with that world. Both poets use the city to describe the sordid surroundings and collapsed values of the post-war years. In Section I of *The Waste Land*, 'The Burial of the Dead', Eliot writes:

> Unreal city,
> Under the brown fog of a winter dawn,
> A crowd flowed over London Bridge, so many,
> I had not thought death had undone so many.
> Sighs, short and infrequent, were exhaled,
> And each man fixed his eyes before his feet.
>
> (*lines 60–65*)

Aldington's Section XXXI ('London by Night') strikes the same note and casts the modern citizens of London as the dead:

> Wrapped in shrouds of white,
> Extended, crouched athwart, uneasy,
> Lie the million breathing corpses
> In their dark funereal cells.
>
> *(lines 1227–30)*

But although Eliot and Aldington share the view of the 'unreal city' as a locus of living death, a kind of hell made manifest, they express their diagnosis of the twentieth century's cultural predicament in very different ways. In order to confront and dissect his own deeply troubled personality and search for answers to his 'murdered self', Aldington employs the three adversarial figures, the narrator 'I', Mezzetin and the Conjuror, in a completely original, moving and illuminating way.

*Fool* may not give a fully satisfactory answer to Aldington's 'murdered self', but he himself saw the poem's conclusion as not without nobility. In a letter to Herbert Read dated the 16th of June 1925 ('Letters to Herbert Read', p. 17), Aldington writes that *Fool* is, in the last analysis, a tragedy and not a satire:

> [S]atire sees man as essentially sordid, but tragedy though admitting that the game is up, grasps at a last hope – an essential grandeur and dignity of man. He is beaten but not ignoble. I tried to show that in the *Fool*. The man is beaten into the mould of a *petit bourgeois*, the most ignominious fate I know; but he has at least the dignity of death, that mysterious adventure, to hold on to. An immortal slave would be an intolerable spectacle; mortality is the last hope, for that last harmony of death is at least silence, repose for the tortured consciousness.

27

That writing *Fool* did not give Aldington 'repose for the tortured consciousness' is evidenced by his satirical war novel, *Death of a Hero* (1929), and short stories, *Roads to Glory* (1930). The bitterness engendered by his war experience was still evident over twenty-five years later in his controversial biography of Lawrence of Arabia (1955). The horrors of war may have faded, but the sense of betrayal and of alienation from the post-war world never did.

## Works Cited

Aldington, Richard, *Exile and Other Poems*, ed. Elizabeth Vandiver and Vivien Whelpton (London: Renard Press, 2023)

Aldington, Richard, *Voltaire* (London: George Routledge, 1925)

Aldington, Richard, *Life for Life's Sake: A Book of Reminiscences* (New York: Viking, 1941)

Aldington, Richard, *The Complete Poems* (London: Allan Wingate, 1948)

Aldington, Richard, *Ezra Pound and T.S. Eliot: A Lecture* (Hurst, Berkshire: Peacocks Press, 1954)

Aldington, Richard, 'Letters to Herbert Read'. Ed. David S. Thatcher, *Malahat Review*, 15 (1970), pp. 5–44

Ancrum, Robin, *A Fool i' the Forest: A Critical Edition*. M.A. thesis (University of British Columbia, 1973)

Cunard, Nancy, *Parallax* (London: Hogarth Press, 1925)

Gates, Norman T. (ed.), *The Poetry of Richard Aldington: A Critical Evaluation and An Anthology of Uncollected Poems* (University Park, PA, and London: Pennsylvania University Press, 1974)

Hughes, Glenn, *Imagism and the Imagists: A Study in Modern Poetry* (Stanford: Stanford University Press; London: Humphrey Milford, OUP, 1931)

Rosenfeld, Paul, *By Way of Art: Criticisms of Music, Literature, Painting, Sculpture, and the Dance* (New York: Coward-McCann, 1928)

Sinclair, May, *The Dark Night* (London: Jonathan Cape, 1924)

Tearle, Oliver, *The Great War, The Waste Land and the Modernist Long Poem* (London: Bloomsbury Academic, 2019)

Vandiver, Elizabeth, *Richard Aldington's Modernist Antiquity: Classics, Imagism, and the Great War* (Oxford: Oxford University Press, 2026)

Whelpton, Vivien, *Richard Aldington: Poet, Soldier and Lover. 1911–1929.*, rev. edn. (Cambridge: Lutterworth, 2019)

Wolfe, Humbert, *Dialogues and Monologues* (New York: Alfred A. Knopf, 1929)

Zilboorg, Caroline (ed.), *Richard Aldington & H. D.: Their Lives in Letters, 1918–1961* (Manchester, New York: Manchester University Press, 2003)

# A FOOL I' THE FOREST

## *A Phantasmagoria*

'A fool! A fool! I met a fool i' the forest!'

# I

'COURT-JESTER to an age that lacks a King.'
Now who said that?
Some fool who thought the crowd should praise his verses
Instead of punting mildly at the races?
No matter. I'll have a jester –
Like a guilty King who hates his thoughts –
To sing, to play the zany,
Show me the world's an idiot's jest,
Cloud-Cuckoo-Land without a Socrates.
When I sit alone                                                  10
Thoughts of ten thousand perished gods
Tease like a letter I forgot to write;
The good man's wisdom
Mads like a buzzing wasp against the pane.
Send me a jester, send me Mezzetin,
Brighella, Feste, Bagatino, Trivelin;
No matter whom, but let him be a fool.

'Las! Good sir, Don Cocodrillo sites in Parliament;
Zirzabella's a Malthusian; Arlequin,
Pale, hungry Arlequin's a bank director,                          20
So ragged and so starved 'twould break your heart, sir;
Pantalone is a reverend judge;
The rest are convicts.

Jupiter was jailed last year for bigamy
And Helen's married to a Guggenheim.
(Sweet Helen, make me immortal with a kiss.)
All lost, all gone, sir, except me,
Poor patient Scaramuccia,
At your service, sir.'

Scaramouch, I hate you.                                        30
You're too fat and clean to be a fool.
Where are your lantern jaw and lousy hair,
Your squint, your grin, your burst-out shoes,
Your miserably squeaking voice that uttered oracles?
I want a fool,
A true, a bitter fool, who's looked at life
And sees it's naught, who knows the rich man's *tare*
That eats into his bosom like a cancer,
Knows where the shoe pinches the lovely dame –
But you're no fool, you're washed and fed;            40
Confess now, on the honour of a charlatan,
You've lectured in America?
I thought as much. Take him away.
I want a fool, a fool, a fool.


## II

*O ch'è cosa bella*
*Andare in barca…*
I'll be my own fool,
Scaramouch is rogue enough to…
Anything, he'll join the Church of Scotland.

> *O guarda nel ciel* 50
> *Innumerabile stelle…*

Damn the stars, they get in peoples' way,
They make girls fall in love
With men that have no money,
They even make men think − a dirty trick,
Immoral, for a good man never thinks.
But I've a plan to thwart the stars;
We'll form a company, we'll buy the sky,
And let it out for advertising,
Large bills by day, electric signs at night; 60
We'll make a fortune and no one then
Will have a chance to think,
Because we'll have all houses made of glass −
The New Epiphany.

> *Chi vuol esser lieto, sia;*
> *Di doman non c'è certezza…*

What's that?
A silly song made by a greasy Dago,
I can't pronounce his name.
Call him Lawrence Doctor. 70
Fancy a banker called 'Lorenzo',
A waiter's name, and singing songs like that;
My God! We have improved since then.

> *Ninetta è sol per Corilo,*
> *Corilo per Ninetta;*
> *Egli vivo e volubile,*
> *Viva ella e legeretta…*

Why do they go about like this at night
Strumming their silly mandolines

And bawling up and down the streets?               80
That's twice they've waked me up,
It'll spoil my stroke tomorrow.
Why don't the police interfere?
I'll make complaints, and if it doesn't stop,
I'll... I'll go back to a decent country
Where a man can sleep
And get a game of tennis quietly.

    *O ch'è cosa bella...*
Nights of Venice! Nights of Venice!
Drifting along the still canals of Venice          90
Hand in hand with Death –
She had red cherries in her hat.
Tintoretto strode along the walls
And Verdi swam with Chinese lanterns
Far out on the lagoon;
A thousand years of garbage underneath
And soft arpeggios overhead,
Drifting music, lips of lovers,
Stars in mist.

Break, break, my heart,                            100
Flow down, my heavy tears,
For Gargamelle is dead
And all the world's too small to bury her.

      *'Twas Venice saw our true love's birth*
      *With soft Idalian song and mirth,*
      *At Oberammergau – Herr Gott! –*
      *I loosed her tender virgin knot.*

Now lies she there...

# III

WE THREE set sail for Athens,
Mezzetin, the Conjuror and I. 110
Mezzetin had broken bail,
So we went with him,
Thinking we might persuade him to come back
And save our money.
But, as he pointed out, and we agreed,
Once they start raking in a man's affairs
God knows what they may find,
Arson, incest, theft, charity and beauty,
Most desperate crimes.

The voyage lasted such an age 120
That I got tired of playing cards
And went and sat upon the poop
And thought of Arethusa's azured arms.
The boat made no advance,
But the pointed seas kept running past,
Monotonous foam churned through the green;
I towed the seagulls on elastic threads.

Thinking of Arethusa turned me grave;
So first I made my will,
And then I thought I'd be an admiral 130
And call my bastard son Horatio;
Afterwards get divorced by going down to Brighton.

Then I was gently sick.

> *Ye mariners of England*
> *That harrow up the deep,*
> *O tell me is my own true love*
> *Adulterously asleep?*

> *How lovely are the Bournemouth bands*
> *That warble on the pier*
> *With here and there a Communist* 140
> *And here and there a peer.*

> *O willow, take me in your arms,*
> *O willow, give me peace,*
> *For I am chasing Byron's ghost*
> *Among the Isles of Greece.*

## IV

WHEN WE got to the Acropolis,
Mezzetin went off to buy some wine.

I wanted to sit down beside the Parthenon
And see the lizards on the broken steps,
And hear the wind among the columns, 150
Arcadian fluting, and look out to sea
To watch for Theseus's sail.
But the Conjurer was obdurate;
He would keep talking of Thucydides
And frightened me with all he knew of Pheidias;

I couldn't interrupt because he'd paid our fares.
Then he kept fanning with his bowler hat
And spouted French:

'O noblesse, O beauté simple et vraie!…
Les Scythes ont conquis le monde…                    160
O Salpinx, clairon de la pensée…
Toi seule es jeune, toi seule es pure.'

I thought he had gone mad and told him so,
But he went on and on.

*Penelope has spun a purple shroud*
*And scattered cypress on her marriage bed.*

*Take up his bones, O lift them tenderly,*
*For they are brittle from the flame,*
*And brittle was his heart.*

*O wrap his bones in purple*                    170
*For a King lies dead*
*And will not come again.*

*O tread upon the violet and the rose,*
*Lay waste the hyacinths among the rocks;*
*He will not come again.*

*O break the silver trumpet and the lyre,*
*Sully the marble, cut the crisped bronze;*
*Byron is dead.*

# V

WHAT'S THAT to me?
My old friend Smut is dead. 180
He made a million out of pork
And sweated bawdy houses.
Rest his soul;
His body lies within the abbey garth.


# VI

THE CONJUROR went on and on;
I thought he'd never stop quotation,
He seemed in such a frenzy;
I recognised Maurras and Tennyson
And Heaven knows whom besides.
All at once he stopped, 190
Clutched me by a waistcoat button,
Shut his eyes and droned out this:

Telemachus grew old and drooled by the fire in the evening,
Paddling with palsied hands in the open breasts of his women
And wetting his oily beard in the wine-cup bossy and golden;
Red embers fell to grey as he mused of the ending of mortals,
The dying groans and the stillness, the funeral fire and the ash.

And he thought how his father Odysseus fared ship-borne far
to the Westward

And came to the dwelling of ghosts and spake with the
  heroes of Troy.
Now fain would Telemachus meet with the ghost of his
  father Odysseus                                           200
To learn the state of the dead, if at last the soul be at peace.


Telemachus rose from his hall and builded a ship most
  stately,
Pitched it within and without and laboured the prow and
  the rigging;
Chose him an hundred feres and stepped up the mast; and
  with shouting
They threshed the sea with their oars and the long ship toiled
  through the waves,
Past the Isle of Calypso and past the land of the lotus
To the dark Cimmerian skies where alone hath Phoebus no
  glory.
In night, under night, through night, they traversed the
  death-dark ocean
Till softly the wet keel struck the sand of a silent shore.


There Telemachus builded three altars and digged them
  about with ditches                                        210
That the hungry ghosts might drink the speech-giving blood
  of the bulls,
That the ghost of father Odysseus might speak to his son of
  the dead.
Now thrice the length of a day they abode in that mortal
  darkness,
And thrice on the darksome soil the victims bled from the
  sword,

41

And thrice Telemachus cried the name of his father
    Odysseus...

But there came no hungry ghosts to lap up the blood from
    the ditches,
There came no sight and no sound, only infinite darkness
    and silence.


# VII

MEZZETIN CAME sweating
And yo-ho-ing up the hill,
So burdened with his parcels and his bottles     220
That he banged his mandoline against the Propylaea
And swore Italian oaths.
He'd bought a pair of horn-rimmed spectacles,
Six litres of white wine and two of red,
And pounds of olives, bread and sausages,
And several heads of garlic.

We had a merry picnic,
Drinking from the wine flasks
And all talking with our mouths full.

Now came still evening on...     230

The pure Athenian air grew dark
Like violet wine that drop by drop
Tints a clear pool.

A rigid dragonfly sank moaning in the sea.

42

The Conjuror threw away his hat
Which changed into a hedgehog and ran off.
Mezzetin looked like a shadowy owl;
Grape-clusters sprouted round his head,
He strummed his mandoline...

> *O Evening Star,*                    240
> *You bring back all good things*
> *The morning stole away...*

The Evening Star that Sappho saw
And Shelley after Plato sang
Droops over London like a tattered flower;
Incense of petrol and of burning coal
Rises to the thrones of Heaven,
Sniffed and snuffled by ungrateful gods.

Pursued by angry bishops out of breath,
The lovers kiss and murmur on the grass,               250
Defying vermin sacred or terrene.

The star that smiles upon the Parthenon
Glares over London like a carbuncle...

Nine million hearts beat on to Bethnal Green.

> *O Evening Star,*
> *You bring the Evening News,*
> *You bring the tired businessman*
> *Back to his tired spouse;*
> *Sappho and Shelley you no longer bring.*

# VIII

THE MOON rose out of Asia –                    260
Anadyomene from the sea.
She wrung the water from her streaming hair;
It trickled down her moving flanks
Dripped from her breast-tips
And her knees.
The shining water splashed about our heads
And washed the Parthenon in silver;
Where it splashed and dripped and tickled
Everything grew splendid; all the rest was dark.
But it poured and flooded over Athens          270
Drowned the houses in its pools,
Lapped swiftly up the hills
And rose about the citadel
Till we were gasping in a flood of moonlight,
Dashing it from flour-white faces
And swimming far above the Parthenon.

After we were drowned
And the coroner had sate upon our bodies,
We rose again,
And found our picnic place                     280
Beneath the Parthenon.

Mezzetin shook the moonlight from his strings
And swayed and nodded as his fingers madly twitched;
Swarms of silver wasps flew upwards

With a buzzing of metallic wings,
Here and there a crimson butterfly
Rose and floated through the heavy air,
Then swooped down and settled on my heart.

Mezzetin sang scraps of foolish verse
But their core, their core was bitter, 290
Pungent to the mouth like pepper.

Now the Conjuror is something of a prig;
He reads too many books
And writes for reputable journals;
He hopes that some day the Academy
(The British one) will make his name immortal.
He got quite angry
And his face
Glowed like a parboiled meteor in the gloom;
He shouted: 'You're a lunatic; shut up.' 300

> *O, we came up to Camden Town*
> *A-riding in a bus,*
> *And Solomon the Israelite*
> *Politely came with us.*
>
> *He hired a hundred char-a-bangs*
> *To take his concubines and boxes,*
> *And told us with a charming smile*
> *That they were grapes and we were foxes.*
>
> *But they whistled the p'lice of Camden Town*
> *And Solomon got took up,* 310
> *Trismyriagamy was the charge…*

45

But there the Conjuror cut him short:
'You're drunk, you bloody fool,
Your nonsense makes me ill.'

Now I like Mezzetin;
Of course he sings most awful rot
And plays his mandoline too much;
But anyone can see that he's a fool,
And such a bitter fool.
So I thought I'd take the Conjuror down a peg.          320
I bawled into his ear:

'Let Mezzetin alone, he's my fool,
And he's not a bore like you.
At any rate his stuff's original,
Not watered William Morris dashed with Swinburne
Like all your drivel about Telemachus.'

I thought he meant to kick me;
Instead he gave a frightful groan
And wept into his fingers.

So we finished up the wine in silence.          330

## IX

THINGS BECAME a little queerer
But the wine had made me brave,
And though the Parthenon kept swaying
And the distant Caryatides waved their arms,
Intuitively I knew they would not fall.

46

Mezzetin kept changing in the darkness.
Somehow he'd thrown off his clothes
And his shoulder blades glowed white in the moon;
Round his head were heavy grapes and vine leaves
And his large eyes shone beneath them                    340
As he softly moved the strings.

The Conjuror was half-asleep,
But he'd changed too;
He looked benevolent and wise,
Fat as a monstrous pear
All buttoned up in clericals.

Then I thought:
'Gaiety's a kind of homage,
So is Mezzetin's fooling,
Yet perhaps the Conjuror was right –                    350
I should have kneeled down
To kiss this sacred earth.
But I hate such demonstrations,
So German and self-conscious.

'What was it that the Greeks had we have not?
Why do we romanticise about them?
Theophrastus gives the game away;
The men of Athens were as base as we,
As dull, as treacherous, as selfish.
Do we praise Pindar overmuch –                          360
The Isaiah of the racecourse?
Could we make poems of a mule race?

'Those Tanagra figurines
Look calm and indolent and graceful
As Gauguin's Tahitians.
They were not tortured by their passions.

'There was something more in Greece
Than tradesmen-citizens and slaves
And graceful flower-crowned girls.
Did they truly reach that harmony we hear of,                370
Balance of thinker, athlete, artist?
Plato mistrusted the imagination;
Pindar's thoughts are clichés
Dressed in splendid robes of gold and purple;
Did the Olympic victors think?'

Mezzetin stopped playing and his eyes were veiled in sleep.

'Yet this Parthenon is harmony,
Science and beauty reconciled with health.
We have beauty that's diseased and wanton,
Art that plays with ugliness and fantasy,                380
Science heavy, technical and mystic,
Stupid health for some – the rest imperfect.

'Lacking harmony, art's a grotesque.
They took the heavy wine of the imagination
And tempered it with snow-cold science.
French art – ragoûts and absinthe.
We have Shakespeare – burn the juniper.
(Yet a Greek would belch at Sophocles.)

'Too soon this harmony disappeared;
Commerce and treachery within,                              390
On one side Roman arms
On the other Eastern myths.
Demosthenes fades to Chrysostom,
Plato to Iamblicus,
Pindar to Gregory of Nazianzus:
Esurient Greeks.

'Mechanics have devoured our art —
Our poets are all journalists, clerks or schoolmasters —
Shakespeare's an ocean-liner,
Donne an aeroplane                                         400
Bumping mysteriously through dizzy clouds.
Our Parthenon's a Jew hotel.'

All was silent.
The shrill grasshoppers were dead.
Harmoniously the stars grouped themselves about the moon.

'Could we slide back and forth through space and time?
Thirty-two per foot per second —
Gravity — the music of the spheres —
Pythagoras discovered strange proportions —
(I must be nodding off to sleep.)                          410
What was I thinking? O yes, harmony.
That's our problem — make a synthesis,
Reconcile the Conjuror with Mezzetin,
Make Mezzetin sing poems instead of nonsense
And make the Conjuror love art and gaiety;
All three live physically like Gauguin's Tahitians.

'Then they'd send us missionaries.'

# X

THAT MADE me think of Hell.

It was like a crematorium
Or rather a Kadaver-factory          420
Where every day
Millions of persons were consumed to smoke.
Out of ten thousand towering chimneys
Gushed black greasy smoke
That whitened to a cloud of banknotes.

On the cloud sat God the Tradesman
Playing at the pianola
'Onward, onward, Christian soldiers';
In an armchair sat his sporty son
Bleating about Newbury races,          430
And winking at the angels underneath.

By the throne stood policemen-lictors
Bearing fasces made of golf clubs.

Miss and Mrs God were calling
In the new Rolls-Royce war-chariot
(Ninety cherubim power, self-starting)
On the Abrahams and Isaacs.

All the Dominations played on Remingtons:
'Glory, glory be to banking!'

All the Powers with Linotypes sang:                    440
'Glory to the laws of commerce,
Praised be Taylor, noble Patriarch,
Praised be Henry Ford, the Prophet,
Praised be Adam Smith, the Saviour.'

All the angels drove to work in tanks.

Showers of wounded grouse fell at my feet.

Far above them all, the mystic symbol,
Made of dazzling electric lights,
Ran about the sky and changed its colours,
Wove its green and scarlet bubbles to the message:    450
'More and More and More for ever,
Holy, Blessed, Glorious Mass Production.'

## XI

MEZZETIN THREW out a coil of melody
By which I clambered back from Hell.
I saw that Hell is the consequence of the hellish mind
And that anyone who will risk his life
Can escape from Hell.
It is useless to denounce the hellish mind
And no one yet has quite explained it.
Moreover, Hell is sometimes useful                     460
If only to reveal its opposite.
If Hell disappeared we might disappear with it.
Perhaps Hell is the only reality
And we are its parasites?

'On Earth we are to enact Hell.'
Why?
On Earth it is better to enact Earth;
We must be men before we're gods or devils.

## XII

THE LACONIAN said:
'O King,                                        470
Poverty is the faithful friend of Greece;
Virtue goes with her,
Daughter of wisdom and good government.'

## XIII

PRAISE AND a crown of glory to the race
Which first shall say: 'We have enough,
Bread, olives, meat, a little wine,
Rough wool dyed purple for our robes;
Now let us live as men.'

## XIV

THE CONJUROR by now was fast asleep.
Mezzetin came nearer to me                      480
And began whispering about Virgil.
All was so hushed on that high rock,
So motionless in still, pure light,
His muffled voice rang loud against my ears.

'Take the sixth eclogue,' he was saying,
'There you have harmony,
Science and myth, charm and austere truth,
Taste, imagination, and a flow
Of verse that holds the heart with beauty.
No need to dwell upon the symbolism –          490
Silenus, the Satyrs and the fairest of the Nymphs –
You know its meaning;
But observe how poetry obeys the laws of science,
How science sways to the rule of poetry.
Not a trace of arid Deism, no metaphysics;
Natural forces and the plastic sense.
Their world was clear and reasonable,
Yet not excluding beauty.
Not for them cowardly wails at death,
But the Evening Star at last          500
Shone out above Olympus.'


# XV

SO HE muttered in my ear,
And half from boredom, half from sleep,
I nodded slow assent.

Then I woke up:
'Saint Paul preached to the Athenians...

'Why try to convince another?
Better to understand him and be silent,
Weigh if his truth relates to yours.

I hate these absolute convictions;                510
What are they but fanaticism?
Your harmony indeed is perfect
But perfection implies intolerance
For all that's not itself.
We are too nervous, too impatient,
Too inconsistent (if you will),
To seek or hold perfection;
What we build today we smash tomorrow.

'Stability, perfection, harmony –
Words that have no meaning for us,                520
Or a far-off, sentimental sound
Like waltzes of the eighties.
We look at all things curiously
And cling to and believe in none,
Not even in ourselves, least of all ourselves.

'Inconsistency's our virtue,
Uncertainty our creed,
Eclecticism our taste;
Don't try to hold us down to anything,
Not even to inconsistency.                        530

'Few have loved Athens more than we –
The pure clear light of Attic thought –
But do not think we always hate New York and London.

'I am compact of whims,
A fellow of the strangest mind.'

He murmured: 'Aguecheek.'

# XVI

MEZZETIN PLAYED rag-time on a banjo,
Clog-danced round the sleeping Conjuror;
Then he nasally orated:
'Ladies and gentlemen, fellow citizens,                    540
This is the famous Parthenon,
The greatest temple in the world,
Built five thousand years B.C.
By Marcus Aurelius and Pericles
In honour of the heathen idol, Pallas Athene.
Although considerably out of date and dilapidated
It has been bought for ten million dollars
By a syndicate of our most cultured businessmen.
Repairs and alterations will be rushed,
And in three weeks this old building                       550
Will be as large and weatherproof
As the Capitol at Washington, D.C.
This, ladies and gentlemen, fellow citizens,
Is another proof of the hearty co-operation
And good-will of the New World to old Eurrup.'

>           *O Pall Athena*
>           *Amurica lo-oves you,*
>           *O Pall Athena*
>           *Here's a han' to you-ou*
>                   *Hoodle-hoo, hoodle-hoo,*          560

*Our biggest high-brows*
*Are nuts on culture,*
*An' our Co-eds are*
*Readin' Homer through,*
　　*Toodle-oo, toodle-oo,*
*Our millionaries are buyin' Euri-pydes too*
　　*Hoodle-hoo, hoodle-hoo,*

*And down in Boston where they bake the beans*
*They know what Happapappazouglos means,*
*So Pall Athena*　　　　　　　　　　　　570
*Here's a han' to you,*
　　*Hoo-hoo-hoo-hoo.*


# XVII

STRIDENT, MENACING, awful,
An owl hooted from the death-still temple,
And the earth shook beneath a mighty tread.
Mezzetin crouched low in terror
And the hair rose stiff upon my flesh;
A tall helmed figure strode between the pillars,
The moonlight flashed from gold and ivory
And the dreadful head burned from the seven-fold shield.　580

Then once more all was still,
And we trembled in the silence.

# XVIII

O pour un moment
que je laisse couler
tout le flot de ma (si belle!) amertume
que je bénisse la Mort
liberatrice bénigne havre fleur du néant
apaisement
à quoi bon se démener?
les hommes sont grossiers les femmes grosses       590
m'ecœurent je suis foutu
je déteste mes semblables
un chrétien me fait l'effet d'un gentil squale
les femmes que j'ai aimées
sont des squelettes peu aimables
voyez le coq qui monte la poule
et vous mangez des œufs
est-ce asses sale l'amour
on me fait voir un avenir sérieux
des avantages considérables       600
mais c'est ton ombre que je cherche
j'ai enterré cette femme
cependant tous mes pleurs se sont séchés
mais il ne s'agit pas de ça
je veux chanter les délices de la Mort
c'est dans un sépulcre fastueux
que je veux goûter mes délices
comme Voltaire à Genève
pensez donc on peut s'y ennuyer en seigneur

*per omnia secula seculorum*
*j'ai ma réponse toute faite*         610
*pour le Jugement dernier*
*au moment où les anges du Seigneur*
*viendront braire dans mes oreilles pourries*
*je leur flanquerai un bon coup au cul*
*de mes pieds osseux*
*d'une voix caverneuse je hurlerai*
*'Chiens savants de l'Eternel*
*voulez-vous bien me foutre la paix?'*

*ainsi je compte achever mes vacances d'infini.*     620

## XIX

*I have worn all servitudes,*
*Have drunk all shames.*

*Sometimes the cruel humour of the gods*
*Exasperates our slavish sycophancy;*
*But we shall never be revenged.*
*When we tear down their last bright curtain*
*We shall find nothing there.*

*They play with loaded dice*
*And when we find it out*
*And draw upon them –*     630
*Lo! They are not.*

# XX

THE CONJUROR awoke and rubbed his eyes,
Then asked why we were cowering there.
When we told him, he only laughed
And wagged a fat fore-finger at us:
'Superstition! Superstition!
Your minds are broken mirrors
And you see the world in inchoate fragments;
You startle at a thousand false reflections,
Children, children!'                                      640

Then he seized a wrist of each of us
And dragged us terror-stricken up the steps
Into the tomb-like temple.

There was nothing except darkness
And a smell of dust and violets;
Fearfully I peered about
Dreading, hoping to see the frowning Goddess
Or the monstrous hooting owl.

Nothing,
Nothing in the darkness but our breathing          650
And the heavy silhouettes of pillars
And the dusty faint smell of violets.

I prayed:

59

*'O Pallas*
*Guardian of the city,*
*Sovereign of this most holy land,*
*Surpassing all in war, in poetry, in strength,*
*Be with us now*
*And bring with you Victory –*
*Clanging down to us on brazen plumes –*        660
*Our friend in strife and battles,*
*Appear to us now;*
*Now, if ever, must you grant us victory,*
*Pallas, O Pallas.'*

Nothing,
Nothing in the darkness but our breathing
And the heavy silhouettes of pillars
And the dusty faint smell of violets.


# XXI

THE CONJUROR broke the silence
And his voice grated in the gloom:        670
'What are these myths but half-truths, quarter-truths,
Dreams of semi-barbarous children
With an exquisite aesthetic tact?
Art is primitive and precedes true knowledge;
The Cro-Magnon, the Cretan, the Ionian
Possessed a subtle art-sense,
But their minds stumbled through crude cosmogonies.
The glory of Hellas is her thinkers,
Not her poets and her artists;
Other races have produced as great an art—'        680

60

(Mezzetin dropped his mandoline with a crash.)

'—But Hellas is the mother of science.
Praise then to Pheidias and Sophocles,
But glory, immortal glory, reverence
To Thales and Pythagoras, Empedocles,
Parmenides and Heraclitus, Aristotle!'

Then he panted, out of breath with shouting.

Mezzetin whispered in my ear:
'Not a word, you note, of Plato;
Ask him what he thinks of *Phaedrus*.'                    690

I whispered back:
'He'd say Plato was a sophist and a poet
In all the mystic dialogues;
The man's an Aristotelian.'
Then aloud:
'When Greek science faltered
Into pedantry and futile subtleties,
Art remained.'

But the Conjuror grasped my arm and shouted:
'It became an art of death,                              700
A stimulus to perverse and jaded senses;
Look!'

At his word a large flat disc of light,
Like Saturn's ring, circled the Parthenon,
Just level with the floor.

On the disc were monstrous visions of lust,
Suetonian bestialities, Caprean orgies, Spintrian chains;
There in bronze or marble in the moonlight,
Gleamed incestuous Myrrha and her guilty sire,
The bestial loves of Leda and Pasiphäe;                    710
Ithyphallic satyrs reeling drunk
Plunged after panting Hyades;
There were Pan and Daphnis, the goat-group from Naples,
Salmacis and the Lesbian Sappho…
Greek myths made tangible for sensual Rome.

The Conjuror shook my arm:
'That orgy of the senses,
That bestiality, that vice –
There is Art uncontrolled by Science,
By love of truth and goodness.'                            720

But I answered coolly:
'The renouncing of all limit is itself a truth.
This boundless orgy, this release of the senses,
This wine-drenched ecstasy,
These Priapic monsters,
Are but a type and figure of human life,
The sensual needs that hold us to the earth.
Even these wildest and most perverse excesses
Are disciplined by a sense of beauty;
Here is no sordid dread of sin,                            730
No Anglo-Saxon cold vulgarity.
Trust me, the pagan orgy had its meaning
And that was, human life.
Despise the senses – even their temporary excess –

And science becomes a vain and arid thing,
A mass of quirks and symbols signifying nothing.
Crush the senses, they take terrible revenge
And waste men's lives, destroy even the earth's beauty.
I do not shrink from those mad orgies;
Share them I cannot,          740
For I am barred from them
By iron habits of race and training;
Neither do I condemn them, but observe.'

The Conjuror threw his arms up with a shriek:
'*Shemah Israel!*'

In a flash all vanished;
Mezzetin and I trembled in blank darkness.


## XXII

GRADUALLY A gleam of half-veiled starlight
Soaked the heavy blackness;
I saw the Parthenon had vanished,       750
Felt dry sand beneath my boots.
I was dizzy and my head ached;
I wondered stupidly at what had happened
And a weight of crime lay on me.
I wished I had gone to Athens care of Cook,
For under his large and brooding wings
The timid tourist is sheltered from all surprise.

I could scarcely see the others in the darkness,

But their eyes shone cat-like and oppressive,
Filling me with superstitious gloom.　　　　760

All that followed is confused,
Blind and wandering like a nightmare,
Uneasy and interminable.

Sometimes one, sometimes the other
Led me by the arm.
We stumbled across a harsh desert
Where the night was loud with rustling wings;
Anubis yelped behind us,
Serpents slid beneath our feet;
We heard the pad of Sphynxes on the sand.　　　　770

Then we wandered for another century
Through winding earthy passages
Cut with innumerable graves.
When my arm was held by Mezzetin
I heard sounds of distant singing,
Monotonous and poignant,
White-veiled women walked beside me
And I was touched to tears by a strange suavity
Compact of resignation, hushed desire,
And eager hope for some unknown good.　　　　780

But when the Conjuror led me
The gloom raged with contending voices
And the clash of steel,
Dull flames glowed in the distance;
All was misery and confusion.

64

I hate to remember this long pilgrimage,
This horrible journey underground
Where we seemed imprisoned in the grave.

At length the darkness lightened;
The roof rose to a round arch,                    790
That in turn soared upwards to a vault
And then we stood beneath a dome,
The mightiest in the world.
Long galleries and naves
Ran off in all directions,
And innumerable silent figures
Prayed or wandered through the twilight.

This vast and murmuring crowd
Was turned in one direction
Where on twisted columns of wrought bronze        800
Sat a cold and mitred god of porphyry,
Grasping in one hand a curious rod.

Knights and women, merchants, ploughmen, sailors,
All in strange and coloured garments,
Pressed forward to the rigid statue
And cast ringing money at its feet.

I could feel that Mezzetin was moved
And would have borrowed from me
A shilling for the idol;
But the Conjuror leaned towards me:               810
'Why do you keep craning round,
Scanning all these passing faces?
Whom are you looking for?'

65

I replied: 'Lorenzo Valla.'[1]

Hardly had I formed the syllables
When we stood beneath a sunny sky,
Breathing air that had no smell of graves.

## XXIII

WE WERE on a hill in some northern country.
From the absence of hedges and game,
The neatness of the distant fields                    820
And one tree-lined road straight as a poker,
I concluded we were in France.

After those centuries of subterranean wandering
And the stifling incense-polluted air
I felt weary and exasperated.
I threw myself angrily upon the ground
And they stood gazing at me
With open mouths and hanging arms.
(Mezzetin, you will remember,
Lost his mandoline in the Parthenon                    830
While I was arguing with the Conjuror.)
I felt so angry with the Conjuror
Because I thought he'd spoiled our trip.
So I attacked him:
'What right have you to spoil our holiday

---

1 'Un humaniste, Laurent Valla (1467) démonstra la fausseté de la donation de Constantin, de la correspondence de Jésus avec Abgar d'Édesse.' Albert Houtin: *Courte Histoire du Christianisme.* (AUTHOR'S NOTE)

Simply because you paid our fares?
You knew I wanted to be happy
And make fun of solemnities with Mezzetin.
He was as gay and silly as I could wish
Until your influence began to work.                    840
Then he got quite didactic
And inspired me with solemn useless reveries.
How can we live like Greeks when we're not Greeks?
What's the use of trying to write like Virgil?
We can't create his sort of beauty
As well as he could, and I hate pastiches;
We must live our own way,
Write like ourselves, not Virgil –
Here I am arguing again! It's all your fault;
And never in my life before                            850
Have I passed through such lugubrious moods
As you've inspired in me.
When I said I wanted a fool,
I meant one merry fool, not two solemn ones.
I loathe all argument and preaching;
Why don't you go away and leave me?'

But the Conjuror replied impressively:
'You can leave us but we cannot leave you
Until you drive us from you;
If we go, we go for ever.                              860
Mezzetin and I are enemies—'
(Here he scowled like Huxley's bust.)
'We were once friends;
That's why we hate each other now.
I know you thought you could reconcile us,

But you can't; you've got to choose;
One of us you can keep
Or you can send us both away.
You know what we stand for; choose.'

I was abashed at this, but answered:                              870
'Look here, when we started out
I was full of gaiety and high spirits,
Ready to take the world and life as jests
And laugh at them with Mezzetin;
But you've destroyed my *verve*
And I'm as dull and solemn as a tired reviewer.
It's true I like Mezzetin more than you,
But one can't spend life only in mocking dullards
Or even in gaiety and music;
One must have something positive                                  880
And that you seem to give me.
If I lose one of you, I'm incomplete;
If both, it's mental death.
Others have reconciled you, why not I?
At any rate I won't choose yet;
Sit down and rest a little here,
And you shall take us on our next adventure.'

Without a word, they sat beside me;
All three of us chewed our bitter-sweet cud,
And mine was mostly bitter.                                       890

# XXIV

O MISERABLE condition of humanity,
Coming from nothing, into nothing going,
Striving with princes and with powers for nothing.
Who indeed would sweat and fardels bear for nothing?
What's a man?
Fortuitous concurrence of whirling electrons,
A problem in mathematics and physics;
Or a divine soul sheathed in clumsy mud
Striving towards God?
We cheat ourselves with words                     900
And only think we think,
Either in terms which analysed mean nothing
Or in terms made arbitrarily exact.
What is Reality?
We start from ourselves,
We return to ourselves;
Each inhabits a narrow chrysalis
He calls reality because it fits his logic;
Outside his universe is the expanse of mystery.
Why should the universe be rational?              910
Why should we say:
It must fit such and such a rule?
That way madness lies and—
Damn my primitive metaphysics.

When we're young, in love, and the sun shines,
Life is delicious; some exuberant force
Plays through our veins,

Everything delights us, all is beauty.
So at twenty, I beheld the Gulf of Naples;
All my being towered into a splendid flame –          920
Sunlight sparkled on the sea
Odysseus cut with carven prow,
And the sirens still were singing.
Every rock-cleft blossomed with narcissus,
Every slope with broom and vine and lemon;
Every hill was sacred to a goddess.
When what mortals call the morning mist
Swept in bright procession from the sea,
I beheld the daughters of the ocean,
Heard their clear song through the scented air.          930
Noon was filled with voices,
Not alone cicadas,
But echoing calls of fauns and dryads
Happy in flower-sweet recesses.
Evening came and like a noble woman
Came the heavenly moon and round her
Glowed the large and silent stars...

Pallid stammering words!
Had I died then life were perfect.
Bitter, bitter-true the saying:          940
'Whom the gods love dies in youth.'
And the gods who loved me sent me Death;
Many months I walked beside her,
Often tempted by her sweet embraces,
Often knowing that a step would make me
Once again that splendid towering flame.
Yes, the gods were kind, but I was cowardly.
Thrice Death clutched me, thrice my will repelled her;

Then the gods abandoned me.
We grow old, the sun grows tarnished;                    950
Life becomes an autumn twilight;
From a lifeless sky rain settles,
Drips from drooping boughs and trickles
Noiselessly from slates and dreary walls...

When the flame goes, man's a husk, a ghost,
Herding miserably with other ghosts,
Sunk in apathy or shrieking at his memories.
That is Dante's 'maggior dolore.'

## XXV

WHAT'S to do then?
For to lament is pitiful,                                 960
Most unbecoming men who strove with Kitchener.

First, the bare bodkin, which perhaps is best;
Then art, religion, science;
Delightful games when played with gusto;
Then the moral philosophy of the ancients –
Plato or Aristotle, Zeno or Epicurus;
Take your choice or take them all
And build a fine new chaos...

> *While Phrygian shepherds watched their flocks*
> *All seated in a mead,*                               970
> *The eagle of the Lord came down*
> *And bore off Ganymede.*

My own ideals are plenty of fishing and rag-time;
I love to feel a fat chub on my hook
Although his carcase dismays and bothers me
And then that Heavenly rag-time:

> *'Are you from Dixie?*
> *Yes, I'm from Dixie!*
> *Well, I'm from Dixie too-oo-oo!'*

Gorgeous, isn't it?                                          980
Such a change from Beethoven and Sousa.
And the joy of dancing to it with a pure, bright girl –

> *There's a hole in her stocking…*

I've sometimes thought I'd be an *artist*;
I'm told they make a *lot* of money,
Not a cubist, of course, but a *real* artist,
Like old Sir Humpty-Dumpty…

But no, there's no solution;
Better go on as before;
Thank God there's no encore after the last curtain.      990

So carry on, Sergeant-Major, carry on.


# XXVI

I SPOKE the last words aloud
And they roused the Conjuror from sleep;
For it was night again.

He stood up and said:
'Get your rifles, men, and come along.'

Mechanically I arose and found my rifle,
Shook my pack and stood by Mezzetin,
Thinking: 'O my God, it's this misery again;
I've often thought I'd wake up from a dream          1000
And find that we were back in it;
Well, it's no sillier than all the rest,
But the slavery of it's dreary.'

It appeared that Mezzetin and I were privates,
But the Conjuror (of course) was Sergeant-Major.
Off we went, to the music of night-firing,
The pleasant evening hymn of Lewis guns
And the pretty fireworks from the line.
The Conjuror led us down a sunken road,
Along the duck-boards of a trench –          1010
As usual I caught my bayonet in wires,
Bashed my iron hat against a bridge
And wrenched my ankles on sixteen broken duck-boards.
At last we reached the frontline;
A quiet relief – only two men hit.

The Conjuror bustled up and down,
Talking to officers and placing sentries;
Mezzetin and I hopped off,
Nipped into the signallers' dug-out
And plotted how to steal the sergeants' rum.          1020
But the Conjuror discovered us and said:
'I want you men to come with me;

73

I'm going on patrol.'
Mezzetin and I gazed wildly at each other;
I thought: 'Now, I know this isn't true –
A Sergeant-Major on patrol!
It must be some dreadful nightmare.'

We went crawling out; the usual thing –
Shell-holes, puddles, sand-bags, knife-rests,
The regulation ration of skeletons, Mark VI.          1030
All went well until we reached their wire;
I could see Mezzetin ahead of me
Caught on a rusty picket festooned with spikes,
Swearing in whispers like a perfect gentleman.
Then that damned Conjuror exclaimed:
'Look out! I see a Bosch!'
Fired his revolver at a stump.
Of course I rolled into the nearest shell-hole;
Up went the Verey lights, down came minnies,
Rifle-bombs, grenades, rifle-fire,          1040
And a beautiful scherzando of machine-guns.

Gradually the concert quieted down;
Suddenly I thought of Mezzetin
And knew he must be dead.
My heart went icy; I felt sick, sick,
And something vital left me for ever.

Then I knew that Mezzetin
Was as much to me as life itself;
I wished a bomb would fall into my shell-hole,
For I felt too numb to stand up to the bullets.          1050

*Who should remember you if we forget?*
*Those who lift top-hats and lay down wreaths?*
*Or those who buried you, dry-eyed and lousy?*

The Conjuror crawled over to my shell-hole.
'Where's Mezzetin?
'Why, dead, of course; what made you fire?'
'Where's his body?'
'Over by that picket, I suppose.'
He stood straight up; I whispered:
'Lie down, lie down, you'll draw their fire.'          1060

Then I noticed a peculiar silence;
Not a gun, a shot, a light;
All was sinister and still.
I climbed from the shell-hole
And we walked towards Mezzetin.
There he lay, dead, dead in mud and blood.
The Conjuror rolled him over, felt his heart:
'Yes, he's dead right enough.'
Then to my disgust and anguish,
He kicked the passive body, muttering:          1070
'I'm glad he's dead;
I always hated and despised him,
With his eternal jingling mandoline
And stupid jokes at high and serious things;
Now he's gone, we'll make a man of you.'

I was aghast and trembling with rage.
Of course I know I should have killed him then,
But I always was a coward

75

And never could face the horror
Of jabbing a bayonet in a man's belly;                    1080
And as usual, my rifle was unloaded.
All I could do was gasp:
'You murderer, you murderer.'


## XXVII

HERE of course should come an elegy on Mezzetin;
But now he's dead I have no interest in writing.
Instead, I'll give you his obituary news.
On a wooden cross in France:
'R.I.P.
012342 Private Mezzetin. I/7 Fools Brigade.
Killed in Action. 1st April, 1917.'                    1090
In the 'List of Casualties':
The same, minus R.I.P.
In the ' List of Recent Wills':
'Sir Hanley Podge, broker, wholesale provision dealer,
Receiver of stolen goods, £1,325,498.
Mezzetin (the famous clown) £1.10 in silver.'


## XXVIII

LOGICALLY, the story ends with Mezzetin's death,
And if it's bored you hitherto,
Think how bored you'll be now Mezzetin is dead.
But life is seldom logical;                    1100
It flows on and on and on,

76

Growing a little dingier every year,
Until it peters out in some inglorious wise.
Mine isn't over yet,
But I must bring this story down to date
As rapidly as possible;
But it's dull, it's dull, it's dull.

## XXIX

SOMEHOW WE drifted back to London.
The Conjuror was quite concerned about me
And even he could see that I was melancholy.          1110
Sometimes he clapped me on the back (a thing I hate)
And cried with hearty cheerfulness (which I loathe,
Because it's humbug, an accepted cheat),
'Cheer up, my son, we'll make a man of you,
Now Mezzetin is dead.'

And I would think:
'Yes, and you're his murderer.'

As I mooned about incapably,
Living extravagantly on my blood money,
The Conjuror grew more concerned:          1120
'Come, you must rouse yourself and act;
Introduce me to your friends.'
I replied: 'I haven't any friends,
But I know lots of people.'
So we went to parties.
Some people said to me: 'How well you look,

Quite manly and set up. Your gratuity
Will come in useful to start you in life.'
Others said: 'Why do you look so odd?
You seem almost demented with misery.'                    1130
I always said the same thing in reply:
'Of course, I'm radiantly happy;
Who wouldn't be, with all you clever people?
But I'm ambitious;
I want to shoot nine politicians,
Fourteen titled tradesmen, two colonels,
One general and a sergeant-major.'
Then naturally they giggled and the women said:
'Oh, *isn't* he too silly?'

The Conjuror was very strong on Knowledge.          1140
He got me a ticket for the British Museum
And made me go there with him
While he did his 'work' –
Thus he pompously described it.
Work! Drivel for the newspapers –
Gagged, except to bawl or simper lies.

You couldn't even smoke there;
So I sat and yawned and dawdled,
Watched the brisk discharge of volumes
From the forty miles of magazine.                          1150
Ennui of knowledge without wisdom
Soaked into my flesh and numbed me.
The Conjuror read on and scribbled,
While I thought of Mezzetin or nothing.

## XXX

ONCE WE met a wealthy tradesman,
Strong and cruel as an Assyrian King.
The Conjuror said something about soldier's hardships;
But the rich man caught him up:

'Hardships? We had hardships too, in England.
One winter – can it be believed? – the government      1160
Rationed my coal, allowed me only one ton a week,
Coal from my own mines too.'

I felt so sorry, so indignant.
Only one ton a week, and from his own mines too!
I felt I'd like to overthrow a government
Capable of such injustice;
And I blushed deeply at the Conjurer's gaffe.

## XXXI

TO AVOID all this I slept by day
And walked about the streets at night;
But the Conjuror came with me,      1170
Gave me good advice unquenchably.

I felt sure there was something I ought to do,
Something rather sudden and bloody,
But what it was I could not think.

Political assassination I rejected –
Useless to cut off one Hydra-head;
Anarchist attacks – futile and cruel;
Bolshevism – a silly tyranny;
Some inbred scepticism destroyed all my plans.
So I walked about the streets at night.                    1180

London before dawn is not uninteresting,
A city given up to sleep and criminals
And slow policemen;
But it's flat and ugly, tiring.

Sometimes as we tramped about
And the Conjuror discoursed intently,
I would think, to put him out of mind:
Behind those dismal house-fronts
Lies a honeycomb of silent cells;
All is motionless, frozen to a seeming death,           1190
Arranged for God to brood over.
There are the boxes for tomorrow's letters,
There sit the typewriters, untouched, in covers,
There lie the files, the tabulated documents,
There are the cleared desks and the minutes
Of yesterday's Board Meeting, rigid, passive;
There are the women's shop-fronts
With their hats and dresses, foolish gew-gaws
Limp and colourless and lifeless,
Lighted strangely by the street-lamps;                  1200
There the empty restaurant windows,
There the jewellers', barred and shuttered,
There the reeking taverns, dark and hostile.

Time glides over them, but does not touch;
Stars peer grimly round the roof-tops;
A tree beside a lamp-post
Trembles with unnatural greenery;
The wood-blocks in the soundless streets
Gleam as if washed in slime;
Dust and dirty paper drift on sinister winds          1210
That titter a ferocious irony
Or gasp a misery not fit for words...

Time glides over them, but does not touch;
Does not touch? Look closer, listen...
There a fissure opened in the brickwork,
There a broken fibre of wood cracked,
There a road-block tilted, oh so slightly,
But it tilted;
There old papers grew a little yellower,
Imperceptibly, but Time is patient.          1220
There a spawn of fungus died,
But Time is patient,
Holds a myriad seeds within her bosom;
There a dead leaf fell, sank slowly
From the stately spreading plane trees;
Time is patient.

Wrapped in shrouds of white,
Extended, couched athwart, uneasy,
Lie the million breathing corpses
In their dark funereal cells.          1230

81

Now if God should speak?
Should plunge the houses
Fathoms deep in earth?

But Time is patient.


## XXXII


ONE MORNING about three o'clock,
Coming back past Waterloo,
We stopped upon the bridge
And I gazed into the water;
More listless and depressed than ever,
Thinking of Mezzetin and Captain Cook,     1240
Dead dogs drifting out to sea,
And Nashe's Isle of Dogs,
And patata and patati...

By now, I'd come to hate the Conjuror,
But most of all his blatant, cheery voice,
So unconcerned with the tragedy of things,
So massively stupid, pyramidally ignorant,
A symbol of the non-perceptive mind –
A thing that makes you stamp with rage
Because it's iron-clad against your scorn,     1250
Padded against the shock and stab of truth
With centuries of crusted humbugs.

There we stood; I brooded sulkily,
While he lacerated my nerves
By lending me a helping hand.

What he said I can't remember clearly;
Something about humanity and work
And sacrifices not in vain,
And getting rid of foolish notions;
Then he quoted some insulting verses                 1260
With a lot of 'ifs', and ended
With his favourite piece of cant:
'We'll make a man of you, my son,
Now Mezzetin is dead.'

This was more than I could bear;
Exasperation lent me wits;
At last I saw what I had to do.
Rapidly I stooped,
Seized him firmly by the ankles,
And, despite his squeals and clutchings,              1270
Splashed him headlong in the river,
Down among the dead dogs and the Roman coins.

I watched the whirlpool disappear
(They never found his body),
Then walked calmly to my room,
Giving each policeman a virtuous goodnight,
Went to bed and slept a heavy sleep...

## XXXIII

EVERY MORNING now at half-past seven
Ethel thumps me in the back;
Up I leap, a loyal English husband,                   1280
Whistle in the bathroom, gulp my bacon,

83

Kiss the children – John and James and Mary;
There's another coming, name not settled –
Buy the morning paper as I hasten to the Tube
And read of all the wonders of the age.

At the office I am diligent and punctual,
Courteous, well-bred, and much respected;
Though the babies are a sad expense,
Every month I save a little money.
Every evening Ethel greets me meekly:                    1290
'Tell me all your joys and sorrows, darling.'

Then I say how Mr Sludge reproved me
For a letter 'not at all in keeping
With this firm's high, honourable traditions';
Or how Mr Hopkinson reported
I deserved promotion for my willing service.
Everything I do is wise and orderly;
My will is made, my life's insured,
The house is being slowly purchased;
Yesterday I bought a family grave.                        1300

Yet,
Sometimes when my stalwart figure
Strides the bleak suburban golf-links;
Sometimes when I lie awake
(Too much coffee after dinner);
Memories of old adventures,
Pangs from the forgotten years,
Haunt me, wound me, tear my heart.

Need I fall so low as this?
Need I prison up my spirit                              1310
In so meek and regular a cage?

Had they lived, had I been different...

Though I quench such thoughts and think of Ethel,
Tell myself that I've been made a Man,
An Empire-builder and a tax-payer;
Miserably mocking voices,
Elf-land flutings, tags of verses,
Scraps of song and distant laughter,
Tinkling of a ghostly mandoline,
Memories of Athens and of Naples,                       1320
Of a life once vowed to truth and beauty,
Pierce me till I start and gasp in anguish...

## XXXIV

*To the palace of the ancient King I come,*
*Leaning heavily upon my staff,*
*Singing one last song.*

*I am but a murmur of words,*
*I am but a dark vision,*
*A dream in the night.*

*O children and ye old men,*
*Lament for the birth of a babe;*                        1330
*Lead on, lead on to the bourn.*

*Farewell, mysterious earth,*
*Farewell, O sea,*
*Farewell, farewell.*

*Now for ever shall my lips be still*
*And for ever my hands be at rest.*

*I flatter no gods with prayer,*
*They are subject and mortal as we,*
*Crushed by inscrutable Fate.*

      *Farewell, mysterious earth,*     1340
      *Farewell, impregnable sea,*
      *Farewell,*
      *Farewell.*

# NOTES

The quotation that serves as an epigraph is spoken by a Fool, Jaques, about his meeting another Fool, Touchstone, in Shakespeare's *As You Like It* (II.7.12). The traditional role played by the character of the Fool in literature is to ignore conventional behaviour, to be outspoken about the truth as he sees it, to be a risk-taker, to indulge in antics that can seem irritating and pointless, to deviate from accepted norms, to speak fearlessly and to make harsh truths palatable with wit and humour. Aldington's Mezzetin displays many of these characteristics. Aldington provided titles for each of the poem's thirty-four numbered sections, but these titles are printed only in the preliminary Contents list and not in the text itself. We provide each section's title here for ease of reference. (In the Contents, the first two sections have the joint title 'Induction. The Crisis'.)

## *Introductory Note*

**'The trio are one person split into three':** This tripartite self irresistibly calls up the Freudian trinity of superego, ego and id. There is no evidence that Aldington had any very strong interest in Freud, but several of his prose writings make it clear that he was conversant with Freudian theory. It seems unlikely that the parallel between the tripartite main character of the poem and Freud's superego, ego and

87

id is purely coincidental, although a Freudian schema does not fully explain the poem's character.

**'Several quotations are woven into the piece':** Aldington says that the two longest quotes he uses are from Aristophanes and Anatole France. The Aristophanes quotation, from *Knights*, appears in Section XX, in translation (presumably Aldington's own). We have not been able to identify a lengthy quotation from Anatole France anywhere in the poem. Aldington greatly admired Anatole France, whom he described as 'a more mellow and poetic reincarnation of Voltaire' (Aldington, *Voltaire*, p. 145). France died while Aldington was writing *Fool* and his Voltaire biography. This final sentence of the introductory Note is omitted in the reprinting of *Fool* in Aldington's *Complete Poems* (1948).

The American edition of *Fool* (Dial Press, 1925) omits the introductory Note. The inside flap of that edition includes quite a different description:

'In this fantasy, under the guise of a fantastic pilgrimage with symbolical characters, Mr Aldington mirrors the spiritual disarray and mental incoherence of our time. We are shown, in fantastic quickly changing vignettes, like the illogical pictures of a dream, the contrast between the ideals of the old Art civilization and the new Trade civilization.

'The piece changes from vers libre to hexameters, from quatrains to rag-time, is satiric, ironic, lyric and tragic, runs from the merest fooling to passages of intense meditation, such as the tragic brooding over sleeping London. The poem breaks through many conventional boundaries but it is held into a sort of unity by the philosophical ideas behind it.'

### Section I: 'Induction. The Crisis'

**lines 1–2, '"Court-Jester to an age that lacks a King". / Now who said that?':** Line 1 is the final line of a poem that Aldington included in a letter he sent to Harriet Monroe (editor of *Poetry Magazine*) in 1922. Gates prints the poem (*The Poetry of Richard Aldington*, p. 208). In his introduction to the 1934 New York edition of his *Poems*, Aldington said that the line popped into his head as he was riding on a train and that it 'suggested the whole' of *Fool* to him (*The Poems*, p. xvii).

**lines 5–6, 'I'll have a jester / Like a guilty king who hates his thoughts':** Perhaps a veiled reference to *King Lear*. Lear's Fool is allowed to present uncomfortable truths to Lear under the guise of jesting.

**line 7, zany:** The first reference to the characters of the Italian commedia dell'arte. 'Zany' is derived from the Italian *zanni*, the name of the stock comic servants in commedia (see OED 'zany', 1a). *Zanni* were known for the physicality of their comedy.

**line 8, 'the world's an idiot's jest':** An echo of Macbeth's '[life] is a tale / told by an idiot' (V.5.26–27).

**line 9, 'Cloud-Cuckoo-Land without a Socrates':** In Aristophanes's comedy *Birds* (performed 414 BCE), the birds join together to form a new city state in the sky, to be called *Nephelokokkygia*, usually translated into English as 'Cloud-Cuckoo-Land'.

Socrates (*c*.470–399 BCE), the teacher of Plato, was a crucially important figure in the development of Athenian philosophy, but left no writings of his own. He appears as a character in Aristophanes's comedy *Clouds* (originally performed 423 BCE; our extant text is a revision of a few years later).

**lines 15–28:** Aldington names several traditional commedia dell'arte characters from which the Narrator 'I' will select the Fool who will accompany him on his phantasmagoria. Their names are given in their English, French or Italian forms.

**line 15, Mezzetin:** This is the French form of the Italian Mezzetino, which means a half-measure of wine. The stock character Mezzetino, one of the *zanni*, is generally portrayed as a skilled musician.

**line 16, Brighella, Feste, Bagatino, Trivelin**: All except Feste are commedia characters, representing servants/*zanni*. **Brighella** is a clever liar and trickster. He is often somewhat older than the other *zanni*. **Feste** is the name of the Fool in Shakespeare's *Twelfth Night*. **Bagatino** is a minor character, known as a trickster. **Trivelin** (or Trivelino) is known for being mischievous and opportunistic.

**line 18, Don Cocodrillo:** A variation of the Capitano figure in commedia, he is a boastful and swaggering soldier. His name means 'Crocodile'.

**line 19, Zirzabella:** An alternative name for the commedia character Isabella, a stock *inamorata* (female lover).

**Malthusian:** one who follows the theory of the English economist Thomas Malthus (1766–1834) that sexual restraint is necessary to prevent the world's population from increasing beyond its means of subsistence.

**line 19–20, Arlequin (Arlecchino):** also called Harlequin. The most famous of the *zanni*, whose name has come to represent the commedia clown in general.

**line 22, Pantalone:** the primary old man character in commedia. In the Anglicised form 'Pantaloon', it means feeble old man; cf. *As You Like It*, 'the lean and slippered pantaloon' (II.7.165).

**line 24, 'Jupiter... bigamy':** Jupiter (Greek Zeus) was the king of the Olympian gods. He was married to Juno (Greek Hera), but was famously promiscuous both with other goddesses and with mortal women.

**line 25, 'Helen's married to a Guggenheim':** In Greek mythology, Helen, the most beautiful woman in the world, was the daughter of Zeus and the Spartan queen Leda. Helen was married to Menelaus, brother of Agamemnon. Her abduction (or perhaps seduction) by the Trojan prince Paris led to the Trojan War, when Agamemnon led an expedition against Troy.

The Guggenheims were a powerful American family whose vast wealth was based on their various mining enterprises.

**line 26, 'Sweet Helen, make me immortal with a kiss':** Quotation from Christopher Marlowe's *Doctor Faustus* (V.1.101).

**line 28, line 30, Scaramuccia / Scaramouch:** One of the *zanni*. He is boastful and sly, but also known for cowardice.

**line 37, *tare*:** In French, *tare* means 'fault' or 'infirmity'. In English, a 'tare' is a weed that grows easily among wheat; see Matthew 13:24–30. The italicisation indicates that Aldington probably intended the French word here.

## Section II: 'Induction. The Crisis'

This section includes several italicised passages that are not clearly attributed to any speaker; see Introduction (p. 23). Here, there is an implication that the songs and poems (some of them identifiable) quoted in Italian are sung by gondoliers, to whom the poem's main narrator, 'I', is listening. See note on lines 78–80.

**line 42, 'lectured in America':** Aldington would lecture in America himself in the late 1930s and early 1940s.

90

**lines 45–46, translation:** 'Oh, what a beautiful thing it is to go boating'. Source unknown. This and the next quotation suggest the songs of gondoliers.

**line 49, 'Church of Scotland':** There is biting irony in the suggestion that Scaramouch, one of the *zanni* of Italian commedia, would join the Calvinist Church of Scotland.

**lines 50–51, translation:** 'Oh, look at the countless stars in the sky.' Source unknown.

**line 64, 'New Epiphany':** The Christian festival of Epiphany, celebrated on the 6th of January, commemorates the Magi's visit to the infant Jesus in Bethlehem. In general, an 'epiphany' means the appearance or manifestation of any god to a human being.

**lines 65–66, translation:** 'Whoever wants to be happy, let him be so; / There is no certainty about tomorrow.' These two lines are the refrain from 'Il trionfo di Bacco e Arianna' ('The Triumph of Bacchus and Ariadne'. This poem was written by Lorenzo de' Medici (1449–92), 'Lorenzo the Magnificent', for the Florence Carnival of 1490. Aldington included this poem in his collection of translations, *Fifty Romance Lyric Poems* (1928, pp. 98–103), where he translated the refrain as 'Then be happy, ye who may; / What's to come is still unsure'.

**line 70, 'Lawrence Doctor':** A literal translation of the name Lorenzo de' Medici.

**lines 74–77, translation:** 'Ninetta is only for Corilo, Corilo for Ninetta; He is lively and fickle, she is lively and frivolous'. This is a quotation from the *Idilli* (*Idylls*) of Aurelio Bertola de' Giorgi (1753–98).

**lines 78–80, 'why do they go about... / bawling up and down the streets?':** These lines imply that the quoted Italian verses are sung by gondoliers, and that the speaker of Section II, 'I', is in Venice. The 'they' referred to in these lines play mandolines as does the character Mezzetin later in the poem, but Mezzetin does not appear as a character until the next section.

**line 90, 'Drifting along the still canals of Venice':** Cf. Aldington's 1915 poem 'Images No. 1', which has the line 'Drifting along the dark canals of Venice' (*The Complete Poems*, p. 38).

**line 93, Tintoretto** (1518–94): Venetian painter. His real name was Jacopo Robusti.

**line 94, Giuseppe Verdi** (1813–1901): The famous Italian composer of operas.

**line 102, Gargamelle:** The mother of the giant Gargantua in Rabelais's five-novel sequence *Gargantua et Pantagruel* (published *c*.1532–*c*.64).

**lines 104–07:** These inset, italicised lines appear to be a spoof of some actual song or poem, but we have not identified a source.

**line 105, Idalian:** Relating to the ancient town of Idalium, a centre of worship of Aphrodite. In Aldington's *Complete Poems,* this was changed to 'Italian'.

**line 106, Oberammergau:** A town in Bavaria, Germany, best known for its Passion Play, first performed in 1634 and still put on in years that end in a zero.

**line 107, 'I loosed her tender virgin knot':** Cf. Shakespeare, *The Tempest,* 'If thou dost break her virgin knot before / All sanctimonious ceremonies…' (IV.1.16–17)

**line 108, 'Now lies she there…':** The hyperbaton here is also the title of one of Aldington's later short stories, published in *Soft Answers* (1932). Here he has made a slight alteration to Antony's line referring to the death of Caesar in Shakespeare's *Julius Caesar*: 'now lies he there' (III.2.131).

### Section III: *'Voyage to Greece – Parody'*

The characters Mezzetin and the Conjuror are introduced in this section.

**line 123, 'Arethusa's azured arms':** A partial quotation from Marlowe's *Doctor Faustus.* Addressing Helen of Troy, Faustus refers to 'wanton Arethusa's azured arms' (V.1.117). Arethusa, an Arcadian nymph, was transformed into a stream as she fled from the river god Alpheus. She travelled under the ocean and re-emerged as a fountain (the Fonte Aretusa) in the island Ortygia in Syracuse, Sicily. Supposedly a cup tossed into the river Alpheus in Arcadia will emerge in the Fonte Aretusa.

**lines 130–31, 'an admiral… Horatio':** the reference is to Admiral Horatio Nelson (1758–1805).

**line 134, 'Ye mariners of England':** These inset, italicised lines begin by quoting the first line of a nineteenth-century ballad by Thomas Campbell. Campbell's verse is profoundly jingoistic, with invocations of Britannia and Nelson, but, thereafter, Aldington undermines the original pomposity with satirical bathos.

**line 138, Bournemouth:** Bournemouth, on the Dorset coast, was a very popular health resort, holiday destination and artists' enclave in the late nineteenth and early twentieth centuries. Its cast-iron pier, completed in 1880, was a well-known feature of the town.

**lines 142–43, 'O willow':** Cf. Desdemona's 'willow' song in *Othello* (IV.3.43–61).

**lines 145–46, 'Byron's ghost... the isles of Greece':** George Gordon, Lord Byron (1788–1824), was one of the major poets of the Romantic period. He died at Missolonghi supporting Greek independence from the Ottoman Empire. His mock-epic poem *Don Juan* includes a bard's song beginning 'The isles of Greece'.

### Section IV: 'Acropolis – Lament for Lord Byron'

**line 146, the Acropolis:** Literally, the 'high city'. The Athenian Acropolis is a flat-topped rocky outcrop 156 metres high. From the sixth century BCE onwards temples and civic buildings were constructed on it, and it provided a refuge in time of siege. It was sacked by the troops of the Persian king Xerxes during his invasion of Athens in the Persian War (480 BCE).

**line 148, the Parthenon:** The most important and famous building on the Athenian Acropolis. It is a temple to Athena that was constructed during the period 447–438 BCE, under the leadership of Pericles (*c*.495–429 BCE), to replace the sixth-century temple destroyed by the Persians under Xerxes.

**lines 150–51, 'And hear the wind among the columns, / Arcadian fluting':** One feature of earlier Imagist practice that can still be found in Aldington's later poems is his use of 'superposition' (the prime example of which is Ezra Pound's two-line poem, 'In a Station of the Metro'). The use of 'superposition' here is a particularly felicitous piece of compression, with the punning association of 'fluting' combining the visual and the auditory – that is, a specific detail of Greek architecture and the aural experience of music. Aldington uses just the last seven words here to fuse both images with great economy. For other examples of superposition, see notes on lines 282–85 and lines 423–25.

Arcadia is a region of the central Peloponnese, associated both in antiquity and in later art and literature with an unspoiled pastoral wilderness. It appears as the home of idealised shepherds, who play their pipes or flutes, in the *Eclogues* of Virgil (70–19 BCE). Cf. note on lines 485–92.

**line 152,'To watch for Theseus's sail':** In myth, King Aegeus of Athens was obligated to send a tribute of seven young men and seven young women to Crete every year, where they were eaten by the Minotaur whom King Minos had imprisoned in the Labyrinth. Theseus, Aegeus's son, led an expedition to Crete to kill the Minotaur. He promised Aegeus that if he was successful he would change the ship's black sails to white so that Aegeus would know as soon as the ship came into sight that his son had triumphed. With the aid of the Cretan princess Ariadne, who gave him a ball of thread to help him retrace his steps out of the Labyrinth, Theseus succeeded in killing the Minotaur. But he forgot to change the ship's sails, and Aegeus leapt to his death from Cape Sounion when he saw the black-sailed ship returning. Theseus thereupon became king of Athens.

**line 154, Thucydides:** Greek historian (*c*.460–*c*.400 BCE). His *History of the Peloponnesian War* is our main source for that war (431–404 BCE), which Athens lost to Sparta, and for Athenian history in the late fifth century BCE.

**line 155, Pheidias:** The greatest sculptor (*c*.480–*c*.430 BCE) of fifth-century Athens. The Parthenon sculptures are attributed to him. His most famous attested works were the chryselephantine (ivory and gold) statues of Zeus at Olympia and Athena in the Parthenon. Neither statue is extant.

**lines 159–163:** These italicised lines are attributed directly to the Conjuror. **Translation:** 'O nobleness of spirit, O beauty, simple and true!... / The Scythians have conquered the world... / O Salpinx, the trumpeter of truth... / Only you are young, only you are pure'. Quoted from Ernest Renan's 'Prière sur l'Acropole' (1883), a prose poem which Aldington has here printed as lines of verse.

**line 160, the Scythians:** Both the Greeks and the Romans used the name 'Scythia' for the area between the Danube and the Don, the Caucasus and the Volga. Classical authors referred to Scythia as a barren wilderness and the Scythians as a stock example of uncivilised savages.

**line 161, Salpinx:** a salpinx was a trumpet-like instrument of ancient Greece. Renan apparently personifies it here through treating it as a proper noun.

**line 164, 'he went on and on':** This implies that the following italicised lines are also spoken by the Conjuror.

**line 165, 'Penelope has spun a purple shroud':** In Homer's *Odyssey*, Penelope, Odysseus's wife, remains faithful to him during his twenty years' absence (ten years at the Trojan War and ten years wandering trying to reach home). During the last few years of her husband's absence, Penelope is besieged by suitors who assume Odysseus is dead and want to marry her. To delay giving them an answer, she says that she must finish weaving a shroud for her father-in-law Laertes. She weaves each day and unravels her weaving each night so that the shroud is never finished. The ruse works for three years until one of her slave women tells the suitors what Penelope is doing.

**line 166, 'And scattered cypress on her marriage bed':** the cypress tree was associated with mourning.

**line 167, 'Take up his bones, O lift them tenderly':** Possibly a reference to Thomas Hood's (1799–1845) poem on a suicide, 'The Bridge of Sighs', which contains the lines 'Take her up tenderly, lift her with care'.

### Section V: 'The Tradesman's Comment'

**line 180, 'my old friend Smut':** It is unclear if Aldington intends a reference to a specific person here.

**line 184, 'the abbey garth':** a garth is a quadrangle surrounded by cloisters.

### Section VI: 'The Voyage of Telemachus'

**line 188, 'Maurras and Tennyson':** Charles Maurras (1868–1952), a French, rigidly arch-conservative, antiparliamentarian monarchist and anti-modernist. There is no identifiable quotation from Maurras in the Conjuror's recitation.

Alfred, Lord Tennyson (1809–92), English poet. The lines on Telemachus that follow are partly based on Tennyson's poem 'Ulysses'. Ulysses is the Latin form of the name Odysseus.

**lines 193–217:** The Conjuror's long recitation, in verse that reflects Greek epic's dactylic hexameter, describes the aged Telemachus's failed attempt to contact the ghost of his father Odysseus. Aldington draws on Tennyson's 'Ulysses' here, but his Telemachus contrasts

95

strongly with Tennyson's aged hero. Tennyson's (and Dante's) Ulysses sets forth on a further voyage to prove his own and his comrades' remaining valour, despite their age, while Aldington's aged Telemachus can only mimic his father's voyage in a fruitless attempt to summon his father's ghost.

**lines 198–99, 'Fared ship-borne far to the Westward... and spake with the heroes of Troy':** In Book XI of the *Odyssey*, Odysseus sails to 'Persephone's land', the entrance to the Underworld, where he speaks with the souls of some of his companions from the Trojan War.

**line 205, 'threshed the sea with their oars':** echoes both a formulaic line in the *Odyssey* and lines 58–59 of Tennyson's 'Ulysses' ('sitting well in order smite / The sounding furrows').

**line 206, 'the isle of Calypso... the land of the lotus':** After his final shipwreck, Odysseus washed ashore on the island Ogygia, home of the goddess Calypso, where he spent seven years until finally Zeus ordained that Calypso must let him go.

The 'land of the lotus' was one of Odysseus's first stopping points after leaving Troy. It was inhabited by the 'lotus-eaters', men who fed on a fruit that caused pleasant forgetfulness of everything. Odysseus had to force those of his men who ate the lotus to continue their journey.

**line 207, 'To the dark Cimmerian skies where alone hath Phoebus no glory':** The Cimmerians' land was close to the land of the dead. Homer says that the sun never shines there and that the land is shrouded in mist, cloud and perpetual night. Phoebus is a name for the Greek god of the sun.

**lines 210–11, 'digged them about... the speech-giving blood of the bulls':** To summon the dead, Odysseus dug a pit and filled it with the blood of a sacrificed ram and ewe. When the ghosts approached the ditch, those whom Odysseus allowed to drink the blood recovered their memories and their voices and were able to speak to him.

**line 215, 'Thrice Telemachus cried the name of his father Odysseus':** In the *Odyssey*, Odysseus spoke to the ghost of his mother Anticleia. He tried three times to embrace her, but she slipped through his arms each time.

## Section VII: 'The Picnic – The Evening Star'

**line 221, the Propylaea:** The ceremonial western gate of the Acropolis, reached by a long winding ramp and flanked on its right side by the small temple of Athena Nike.

**line 230, 'Now came still evening on':** A quotation from Milton, *Paradise Lost*, IV.598.

**lines 231–32, 'The pure Athenian air grew dark / Like violet wine':** The poet Pindar (*c*.518–*c*.438 BCE) calls Athens 'shining and violet-crowned' (Fragment 76). Cf. Eliot's 'the violet hour, the evening hour that strives' (*The Waste Land*, line 220; see also *The Waste Land* lines 215, 372, 379).

**line 237, 'A shadowy owl':** The owl is an attribute of Athena.

**line 238, 'Grape-clusters sprouted round his head':** This description assimilates Mezzetin to Dionysus, the Greek god of wine.

**line 239, 'He strummed his mandoline':** This may indicate that Mezzetin sings the following italicised lines and lines 255–59 as well.

**lines 240–42, 'O Evening Star...':** These lines of verse and the expanded version at lines 255–59 are a pastiche of lines by Sappho (*c*.630–570 BCE): 'Hesperus, bringing all the things that shining Dawn scattered, you bring the sheep, you bring the goat, you bring the child back to the mother' (fr. 104a). Hesperus was the evening star. On Sappho, see note on line 714.

Cf. *The Waste Land*, 'the violet hour' passage (lines 220–23); Eliot's note indicates that he intended a reference to the Sappho poem here.

**line 244, 'Shelley after Plato sang':** Percy Bysshe Shelley (1792–1822), English Romantic poet. This refers to the last line of his poem 'Evening, Ponte Al Mare, Pisa' and to his four-line 'Epigram 1: To Stella, from the Greek of Plato', which compares its subject to the morning star while she lived and to the evening star now that she is dead. The name 'Stella' is Latin for 'star'.

**line 248, 'snuffled by ungrateful gods':** The Olympian gods delighted in the savour of smoke rising from burnt offerings.

**line 255–56, 'O Evening Star, / You bring the Evening News':** 'The Evening Star' was a long-running (1881–1980) and highly popular London evening newspaper. Cf. T.S. Eliot, 'The Boston Evening Transcript', lines 3–5.

*Section VIII: 'Moonrise – King Solomon – The Conjuror as Poet'*

**line 261, 'Anadyomene from the sea':** 'Anodyomene' is a term normally applied to Aphrodite. 'Aphrodite Anadyomene' is an ancient statue type in which the nude goddess wrings water from her hair as she rises from the sea. Aldington gives an effective ekphrasis of the Anadyomene type, although transferring the imagery to the moon.

**lines 282–85:** Another example of superposition (cf. notes on lines 150–151 and 423–425). The movement of the player's fingers releases light from the strings. This visual effect precedes the sound of the music, as a silvery shimmer metamorphoses into buzzing insects.

**lines 301–04, 'Oh, we came up to Camden town':** Perhaps a spoof of the folksong 'Oh, we came up from Somerset'. Probably sung by Mezzetin; see note on line 312.

**line 303, 'Solomon the Israelite':** Solomon, son of David, was the fourth king of Israel and Judah, who reigned in the tenth century BCE (see 2 Samuel, 1 Kings and 2 Chronicles). He built the first temple in Jerusalem and was renowned for his wisdom.

**line 305, 'char-a-bangs':** a humorous distortion of *charabanc*, 'bus'. In the *Complete Poems* this is emended to *char-à-bancs* (p. 204).

**line 308, 'they were grapes and we were foxes':** A reference to Aesop's fable. A fox who cannot jump high enough to seize a bunch of grapes comforts himself by declaring that 'the grapes are sour, anyway.'

**line 311, 'Trismyriagamy was the charge':** an invented word, using Greek terms, meaning 'marrying thirty thousand wives'. According to the Bible, Solomon had 700 wives and 300 concubines (1 Kings 11:3).

**line 312, 'the Conjuror cut him short':** An indication that the 'Oh, we came up to Camden town' passage is sung by Mezzetin.

**line 325, 'William Morris dashed with Swinburne':** William Morris (1834–96), English poet, artist and socialist activator. He translated the *Odyssey* into rhymed hexameter couplets.

Algernon Charles Swinburne (1837–1909), English poet, playwright and critic, known for his metrical skill and his vivid imagery.

*Section IX: 'Greek Art – The Conflict and Reflections'*

**line 334, 'the distant Caryatides waved their arms':** Caryatids are columns carved as statues of robed women. The most famous ones are on the porch of the Erechtheum, directly opposite the Parthenon on the Acropolis. 'I' is hallucinating here, since the Caryatids of the Erechtheum have no arms; theirs have broken off over the centuries. Even the best preserved Caryatid, brought to London by Lord Elgin and still in the British Museum, is armless.

**line 339, 'heavy grapes and vine leaves':** Mezzetin is again given the attributes of Dionysus.

**line 357, 'Theophrastus gives the game away':** Theophrastus (*c*.370–*c*.287 BCE) was an associate of Aristotle and his successor as head of the Lyceum. His interests were wide ranging, covering logic, philosophy, rhetoric and science. The reference here is to his *Characters*, in which he identifies (unfavourably) the traits of thirty different personality types. Aldington translated *Characters* in 1924. On Aristotle, see note on line 685.

**lines 360–62, 'Pindar... / poems of a mule-race':** Pindar wrote odes for victors in the athletic contests at the Olympian, Pythian, Isthmian and Nemean Games. These contests included chariot races, with two-mule and four-horse chariots.

**line 363, 'Tanagra figurines':** Tanagra was a city in Boeotia. Numerous terracotta figurines were excavated from its cemeteries in the nineteenth century. They are naturalistic representations of everyday life, many depicting lavishly dressed women, which often retain their original pigmentation.

**line 365, 'Gauguin's Tahitians':** Paul Gauguin (1848–1903), French Post-impressionist painter who spent several years in Tahiti.

**line 372, 'Plato mistrusted the imagination':** Plato (*c*.429–347 BCE), one of the greatest ancient philosophers, was a pupil of Socrates. Plato's writings cover a large range of topics, including among others philosophy, ethics, rhetoric, poetry and justice. His most fundamental doctrine teaches that there is a crucial distinction between the material world perceived by our senses and 'reality', which is a world of eternal 'Forms' (of Beauty, Justice, Truth, etc.). In *The Republic*, Plato excludes poets from the ideal state due to his 'mistrust of the imagination'.

Plato's works are written in dialogue form. The question of how much the views of the Platonic character 'Socrates' align with the teachings of the actual Socrates and how much they are Plato's own theories remains vexed. On Socrates, see note on line 9.

**line 373, Pindar's thoughts:** On Pindar, see notes on lines 231–32.

**line 388, Sophocles (*c*.496–406 BCE):** One of the three great Athenian tragedians (along with Aeschylus and Euripides) of the fifth century BCE. Seven of Sophocles's 120 plays have survived: *Ajax, Antigone, Electra, Oedipus at Colonus, Oedipus the King, Philoctetes* and *Trachiniae.*

**line 391, 'Roman arms':** Rome was victorious over Greece in the Battle of Corinth (146 BCE), at which point Greece became part of the Roman Empire.

**line 392, 'Eastern myths':** Almost certainly a reference to Christianity, which Aldington saw as a malign influence on classical culture. The apostle Paul preached in Athens, probably in 50 or 51 CE.

**line 393, 'Demosthenes fades to Chrysostom':** Demosthenes (384–322 BCE) was the greatest Athenian orator. His extant speeches are rhetorical masterpieces and an invaluable source of information about Athenian political history in the fourth century BCE. His most famous speeches, the 'Philippics', were directed against Philip of Macedon (382–336 BCE) and his military campaigns against Greece.

The sobriquet 'Chrysostom' means 'golden-mouthed' and refers to eloquence. Two ancient figures were commonly given this title; either of them would fit the context here. Dio Chrysostom (*c.*40–115 CE) was a Roman-era orator, so the comparison to Demosthenes would indicate the decline of oratory. Alternatively, Aldington may mean the Christian saint, John Chrysostom (*c.*349–407); this comparison of a classical orator to a later Christian would parallel the comparison of Pindar to Gregory of Nazianzus in line 395.

**line 394, 'Plato to Iamblicus':** On Plato, see note on line 372. Iamblichus (*c.*242–*c.*325 CE) was a Syrian Neoplatonist and pagan theologian.

**line 395, 'Pindar to Gregory of Nazianzus':** On Pindar, see note on lines 231–32. Gregory of Nazianzus (*c.*329–90 CE), Archbishop of Constantinople in 380–81, was one of the most important theologians of the fourth century, especially in his views on the Trinity. He was an extremely accomplished rhetorician who was trained in classical rhetoric.

**line 400:** John Donne (1572–1631), English metaphysical poet.

**line 402, 'Our Parthenon's a Jew hotel':** In this section of his criticism of modern society, 'I' draws on the antisemitic trope of the rich and vulgar Jewish businessman, common at this period.

**lines 408–09, 'the music of the spheres – / Pythagoras discovered strange proportions':** Pythagoras of Samos (b. mid sixth century BCE) was a religious sage, mathematician, musical theorist and astronomer. He supposedly taught that the heavenly bodies (planets, sun, moon, stars) moved in their specific spheres according to mathematical equations that correspond to musical harmonic proportions, and that these spheres' motions produced a music. It is unknown how many of the doctrines and theorems attributed to him were actually his, and how many were developed by his later followers.

## Section X: 'The Vision of Hell'

**line 420, 'a Kadaver-factory':** a reference to the propagandistic rumour during WWI that the Germans were cooking down dead bodies for their fats.

**lines 423–25:** A third example of superposition (cf. notes on lines 150–51 and 282–85).

Aldington uses superposition satirically here in a section that focuses on the sordid industrialism and profit-making of contemporary London. In a hallucinatory transformation industrial pollution in the form of belching smoke becomes a shower of five-pound notes (at the time these were printed on white paper).

**line 427, pianola:** Also called a player piano.

**line 428, 'Onward, Christian soldiers':** A popular hymn by Sir Arthur Sullivan (1842–1900).

**line 430, 'Newbury races':** The racecourse in Newbury, Berkshire, is just five miles from Hermitage, where Aldington lived in 1920, so he would be well aware of any race meetings held there.

**lines 432–33, 'policemen-lictors… fasces made of golf clubs':** Lictors were the attendants who accompanied Roman magistrates. Each lictor carried a *fasces*, a bundle of elm or birch rods topped with a single-headed axe, which served as a visual representation of the magistrate's power.

**lines 434–37, 'Miss and Mrs God were calling / In the new Rolls Royce… / On the Abrahams and Isaacs':** See note on line 402.

**lines 438–40, 'Dominations… Powers':** Cf. Milton, *Paradise Lost*, V.600–01, 'Hear all ye angels, progeny of light, / Thrones, Dominations, Princedoms, Virtues, Powers', and Colossians 1:16, 'By Him were all things created… whether they be thrones or dominions or principalities or powers' (KJV).

**line 438, Remingtons:** a brand of typewriter.

**line 440, linotypes:** A kind of typesetting machine, which set an entire line of type at a time. It was widely used from the late nineteenth century until it was largely replaced by digital typesetting in the late twentieth century.

**line 442, Taylor:** Frederick Winslow Taylor (1856–1915), American mechanical engineer. His 1909 book *The Principles of Scientific Management* was extremely influential on the development of industrial engineering. He made his personal fortune through developing and patenting methods of processing steel.

**line 443:** Henry Ford (1863–1947), American industrialist who founded the Ford Motor Company in 1903. In 1908 he introduced the Model T automobile, priced to be affordable to middle-class buyers.

**line 444:** Adam Smith (1723–90), Scottish philosopher and economist. His book *The Wealth of Nations* (1776) is a foundational work of modern economic theory.

**line 446, 'showers of wounded grouse fell at my feet':** The grouse-shooting season in the UK begins on the twelfth of August, traditionally referred to as 'the Glorious Twelfth'. The birds are chased into flight by 'beaters' and then shot by lines of waiting hunters, making grouse-hunting an evocative image of mass slaughter.

*Section XI: 'The Escape from Hell – Reflections'*

**line 465, 'On Earth we are to enact Hell':** Cf. Friedrich Hölderin (1779–1843), 'Immerhin hat das den Staat zur Hölle gemacht, daß ihn der Mensch zu seinem Himmel machen wollte' ('Nevertheless, the state, which man wanted to make his heaven, has been made into a hell'; *Hyperion* Book 1, VII).

*Section XII: 'Spartan Dignity'*

**lines 469–73, 'The Laconian said...':** Laconian means Spartan. According to the account by the historian Herodotus (*c*.484–*c*.425 BCE), the exiled Spartan king Demaratus accompanied Xerxes on his expedition against Greece in 480 BCE and acted as his advisor. When Xerxes asked about the Greeks' ability to resist the Persian onslaught, Demaratus replied that 'Poverty is Greece's constant companion, but their *aretē* [manliness; courage; virtue] comes from wisdom and strong law' (VII.102).

### Section XIII: 'Praise of Non-Commercial Races'

**lines 475–78, 'We have enough... live as men':** We have not identified a source for this quotation.

### Section XIV: 'Virgil'

**line 481, Virgil:** Publius Vergilius Maro (70–19 BCE). Roman poet, best known today as the author of *The Aeneid*. He also wrote *The Eclogues* and *The Georgics*. He was the most famous and widely read Roman poet in late antiquity, the middle ages and into the modern period.

**lines 485–92, 'Take the sixth eclogue':** Eclogue VI recounts that two boys, Chromis and Mnasyllos, happened upon the sleeping god Silenus, the aged and inebriated companion of Bacchus. Joined by the Naiad Aegle, they bound Silenus and required him to sing for them. Silenus's song describes the creation of the world from the void and the creation of human beings; he then summarises several Greek myths, focusing on stories of unhappy or unnatural loves and transformations of humans into plants or animals.

### Section XV: 'Ancient Harmony – Modern Incoherence'

**line 506, 'Saint Paul preached to the Athenians':** The apostle Paul delivered the Areopagus sermon in Athens; it is recorded in Acts 17: 16–34.

**line 532, 'the pure clear light of Attic thought':** Attica is the region in which Athens is located.

**lines 534–36, 'Aguecheek':** Sir Andrew Aguecheek is a slow-witted, vain and buffoonish character in Shakespeare's *Twelfth Night*. Aldington combines Aguecheek's line 'I am a fellow o' th' strangest mind i' th' world' (I.3.110–11) with Theseus's comment 'The lunatic, the lover and the poet / Are of imagination all compact' (*Midsummer Night's Dream* V.1.7–8)

### Section XVI: 'The Yankee Orator – The Culture Hymn'

Both Eliot and Aldington use ventriloquism (in the 'Game of Chess' section of *The Waste Land*, Eliot gives a convincing approximation of cockney chatter in a London pub). Aldington allots the mock-role of an incompetent tourist guide at the Parthenon to Mezzetin, who is made to speak in a parodic American accent (Aldington might be echoing the character of Ezra Pound's speech here).

**line 543, 'Built five thousand years B.C.':** The 'tour-guide' here confuses 5000 BCE with the fifth century BCE. The Parthenon was constructed during the period 447 to 438 BCE.

**line 544, 'Marcus Aurelius and Pericles':** Another confusion of dates, and of cultures. Marcus Aurelius, a Roman emperor (121–80 CE), died nearly 600 years after Pericles.

**line 545, 'heathen idol, Pallas Athene':** Pallas is Athena's most common epithet. Athene is an alternative spelling of Athena.

**lines 556–72:** Since Mezzetin's 'nasal oration' is closed by a quotation mark at the end of line 554, it is unclear who speaks – or sings – this italicised passage (see Introduction, p. 24).

This 'Culture Hymn' is reminiscent of the 'Shakespeherian Rag' passage in Section II of *The Waste Land* (lines 128–30), in which Eliot spoofed an actual song. We have been unable to identify any song as an overall model for the Culture Hymn, but 'Toodle-Oo' was the title of a popular song of 1923, from the musical comedy *Mary Jane McKane* (lyrics William Cary Duncan and Oscar Hammerstein II, music Herbert Stothart and Vincent Youmans). However, the lyrics of this song in no way resemble Aldington's 'Culture Hymn'.

**line 566, 'Euri-pydes':** Euripides (*c*.480–406 BCE) was one of the three great tragedians of fifth-century Athens, along with Aeschylus and Sophocles. The spelling here represents a mispronunciation of the name.

**line 569, Happapappazouglos:** A nonsense word, apparently Aldington's own invention, mimicking similar nonsense words in Aristophanes's comedies.

### Section XVII: 'The Manifestation of Pallas'

**line 574, 'An owl hooted':** The owl was one of Athena's standard attributes.

**lines 578–79, 'A tall helmed figure... gold and ivory':** This is a reference to Pheidias's chryselephantine statue of Athena that stood in the Parthenon.

**line 580, 'the dreadful head burned from the seven-fold shield':** Pheidias's statue is not extant but there are many small-scale copies of it, which show that Athena's shield featured the head of Medusa in its centre.

## Section XVIII: 'Death'

This section is the passage Aldington refers to in the Introduction to his *Complete Poems*, where he says that 'There is one passage of *A Fool i' the Forest* written in French because it happened to come that way' (*The Complete Poems*, p. 16).

No speaker is identified or implied for this section. Its use of the first person singular might suggest that 'I' is the speaker, but if so this is the only passage where 'I' uses a language other than English.

The passage can be translated as:

'Oh just for a moment
let me pour forth
the complete flood of my (so beautiful!) bitterness                585
let me bless freedom-giving Death
that benign haven that blossom of nothingness
a sense of calmness
why continue to struggle?
men are coarse and fat women                590
disgust me I am damned
I detest my fellow men
a Christian makes me think of a well-meaning shark
the women whom I have loved
are unappealing skeletons                595
just see how the cockerel mounts the hen
and you eat eggs
is love so filthy
I am made to envisage a serious future
with considerable advantages                600
but it's your ghost I am looking for
I have buried this woman
however my tears have completely dried up
but that's not the point
I wish to sing the delights of Death                605
it is in a lavish tomb
that I wish to savour all my delights
like Voltaire in Geneva
just think one can be bored in a lordly manner

for eternity                                                    610
I have my answer ready-made
for the Last Judgment
just as the angels of the Lord
come to bray in my decomposed ears
I'll give them a good kick up the arse                          615
with my bony feet
and in a hollow voice I shall yell
"Performing dogs of the Eternal
will you please leave me alone?"
That is how I plan to spend my endless holidays.'              620

**lines 607–08, 'je veux goûter mes délices / comme Voltaire à Genève:** 'Les Délices' was the name of the house (now the Voltaire Museum) in Geneva where Voltaire lived from 1756–60, when he was escaping the pursuit of the French authorities.

**line 610, *per omnia secula seculorum*:** Literally, 'through all ages of ages'. This phrase appears in the Latin Mass.

**lines 618–19, 'Chiens savant de l'Eternel / voulez-vous bien me foutre la paix?':** Perhaps an adaptation of words Voltaire supposedly spoke on his deathbed, addressed to a priest who asked if he recognised the divinity of Jesus Christ: 'For God's sake, let me die in peace' (*Voltaire*, p. 124). Aldington was working on his study of Voltaire at the same time that he was writing *Fool*.

## Section XIX: 'The Gods'

Here, as in the previous section, no speaker is identified for these italicised lines.

**line 621–2, 'I have worn all servitudes, have drunk all shames':** Cf. François Villon, 'Le Testament', I.1–2: 'En l'an de mon trentiesme aage, / Que toutes mes hontes j'euz beues' ('In the thirtieth year of my age, / When I had drunk all my shames'). Aldington admired Villon and had translated his 'Ballade des pendus' (as 'Epitaph in Ballad Form') in *Exile and Other Poems* (1923; reprinted in *Fifty Romance Lyric Poems*, 1928).

**line 628, 'They play with loaded dice':** Cf. Sophocles fr. 895: 'Zeus's dice-throws are always lucky'.

## Section XX: 'The Empty Shrine'

**lines 645, 652, 668, 'smell of violets':** See note on lines 231–32.

**line 653, 'I prayed':** This is an unparalleled attribution to 'I' of an inset, italicised quotation.

**lines 654–64, 'O Pallas / Guardian of the city…':** This is the quotation from Aristophanes to which Aldington refers in his introductory Note. These lines are a fairly close translation of Aristophanes's *Knights*, 581–94 (produced 424 BCE).

**line 659, 'bring with you Victory':** Athena was the patron goddess of Athens and the goddess of war. The upper-case 'V' in Victory here probably indicates the personification of victory as the goddess Nike.

## Section XXI: 'Greek Science – Pagan Sensuality'

**line 675, 'The Cro-Magnon, the Cretan, the Ionian':** The Cro-Magnons were the first early modern humans to settle in Europe from western Asia 56,000 years ago. 'The Cretan' refers to ancient Cretan 'Minoan' civilisation. The ruins of the most important Minoan palace complex, at Knossos, were excavated by Sir Arthur Evans from 1900–1931. His findings included many exceptional works of art, especially frescos from the palace walls. Ancient Ionia, a region of western Turkey, was culturally and linguistically Greek. In the sixth century BCE a group of pre-Socratic philosophers flourished in Ionia. Their interests included scientific as well as philosophical speculation and theories.

**line 685, Thales, and Pythagoras, Empedocles:**

Thales of Miletus, in Ionia; *c*.624–*c*.545 BCE. He was considered one of the 'Seven Sages' of antiquity and one of the most important pre-Socratic philosophers. His works have all been lost. According to Aristotle, he taught that water is the first principle of all things (Aristotle *Metaphysica A 3, 983*$^b$20ff). He was also a mathematician and astronomer. Herodotus credited him with calculating the height of the Egyptian pyramids and predicting an eclipse of the sun in May 535 BCE (1.74.2). On Aristotle, see note on line 685.

Pythagoras: See note on lines 408–09.

Empedocles of Acragas (modern Agrigento), in Sicily; *c*.492–432 BCE. Surviving fragments of his writings show that he developed a theory that the material world was constituted by four elements, or basic forms of matter (earth, air, fire and water). Those elements interacted with one another under the influence of two powers, Love and Strife, in repeated world cycles, depending on whether Love or Strife was dominant. His theory of the elements was probably a direct response to Parmenides; see on line 685.

**line 686, Parmenides and Heraclitus, Aristotle:**

Parmenides and Heraclitus were both pre-Socratic philosophers. Parmenides of Elea wrote in the late sixth or early fifth century BCE. His work 'On Nature' (a poem in dactylic hexameter), which survives in large fragments, argued that reality is unified and unchanging, and that seeming changes in the material word are only matters of appearance.

Heraclitus (fl. fifth century BCE) of Ephesus argued for the primacy of *logos* (reason, discourse, thought) in the universe and for the central role of change for maintaining the order of the material world. His work survives only in fragments; his best known aphorisms, 'One cannot step into the same river twice' and 'Everything flows' (*panta rhei*) both highlight his concept of change.

Aristotle (384–322 BCE), born in Stagira, came to Athens at the age of seventeen, where he studied at Plato's Academy until Plato's death (347 BCE). Aristotle became the most influential ancient philosopher after Plato; his writings are often critical of or opposed to Plato's. His works ranged over philosophy, logic, ethics, political theory, literary criticism, rhetoric and science, and were incalculably influential on later European thought.

**line 689:** On Plato, see note on line 372.

**line 690, *Phaedrus*:** One of Plato's dialogues. In it, Socrates discusses the nature of love, divine madness, the immortality of the soul, reincarnation, poetry and rhetoric. The dialogue includes the famous allegory of the charioteer, depicting the human soul as tripartite, with a charioteer representing intellect, one of the horses representing the rational and moral impulses, and the other horse representing the irrational appetites and passions. The parallels to the Conjuror, Mezzetin and 'I' are obvious. Plato's theory of the tripartite soul appears elsewhere as well, most notably in *Republic* Book 4.

**lines 692, 'a sophist':** The Sophists were a group of fifth-century BCE itinerant teachers and philosophers. Their writings have not survived. Plato and (apparently) Socrates were strongly opposed to their positions, which they saw as espousing a dangerous moral relativism.

**'a poet':** Plato was also wary of poetry. His arguments against poetry are complex, but among other points he considered it dangerous because it was based in falsehood, distracted attention from reality and aroused emotions that should be controlled rather than encouraged. Cf. note on line 372.

**line 693, 'the mystic dialogues':** Several of Plato's dialogues deal with metaphysical questions such as the nature of reality, the immortality of the soul, the Theory of the Forms and so on.

**line 707, 'Suetonian bestialities, Caprean orgies, Spintrian chains':** Refers to the supposed proclivities of the Roman emperor Tiberius. According to the Roman historian and biographer Suetonius (*c*.69–*c*.122 CE), Tiberius frequently indulged in orgies in his palace on Capri (*Life of Tiberius* 43). These orgies featured, among other things, simultaneous copulation 'in a triple connection' (*triplici serie conexi*); Suetonius says that Tiberius called the participants in these activities *spintrias*.

**line 708, 'in bronze or marble':** Although he specifically refers to only two statue groups (see on line 712), Aldington apparently pictures all of these scenes as represented in sculpture.

**line 709, 'incestuous Myrrha and her guilty sire':** According to Ovid's *Metamorphoses* (10.298–502), Myrrha committed incest with her father Cinyras. Their son was Adonis.

**line 710, 'Leda and Pasiphae':** Leda, queen of Sparta, was seduced by Zeus, who appeared to her in the form of a swan. Their daughter was Helen (see note on line 25). Pasiphae, wife of King Minos of Crete, was smitten with passion for a bull. The craftsman Daedalus built a wooden cow in which she could crouch and mate with the bull. Their son was the Minotaur, half bull and half man, whom Minos imprisoned in the Labyrinth and who was slain by Theseus (see note on line 152).

**lines 711–12, 'Ithyphallic satyrs reeling drunk... / panting Hyades':** Satyrs were the mythical followers of Dionysus, normally depicted in ancient art as ithyphallic (i.e. with erect penises). In Greek art, they are usually shown as humans with animal tails and sometimes ears. Fauns, their Roman equivalent, are usually portrayed with the legs and feet of goats.

The Hyades were a group of nymphs who brought rain, often described as the daughters of Oceanus. Satyrs were widely depicted pursuing nymphs, but had no specific connection with the Hyades in particular.

**line 713, 'Pan and Daphnis, the goat-group from Naples':** This refers to two ancient statue groups. Pan was a god of the rustic countryside, often depicted as a goat from the waist down (like a Roman faun). In a statue group in the Uffizi, Pan sits with his arm around the young shepherd Daphnis, who is holding a set of 'pan-pipes'. The 'goat-group from Naples' was found at Pompeii and is now in the Naples Archaeological Museum. Pan – or perhaps a satyr – is copulating with a recumbent goat.

**line 714, 'Salmacis, and the Lesbian Sappho':** Ovid's *Metamorphoses* describes the nymph Salmacis's passion for the boy Hermaphroditus, which led to the two of them being conjoined permanently into a form that was both male and female (4.285–388).

Sappho (sixth century BCE) was one of the greatest poets of the ancient world and the most renowned of women poets. Her work survives only in fragments, apart from one apparently complete poem. Many of her poems describe the beauty of other women and indicate Sappho's love for them, but none of her work is erotically explicit. The modern term 'Lesbian' derives from the fact that she was from Lesbos.

**line 725, 'Priapic monsters':** Priapus was a Roman god of fertility and male sexuality, normally portrayed with an enormous erect phallus. He was a guardian of gardens in particular, where his statues often stood, and of houses.

**line 736, 'signifying nothing':** Cf. Macbeth's characterisation of life as 'a tale / Told by an idiot, full of sound and fury, / signifying nothing' (V.5.29–31).

**line 743, 'Neither do I condemn them':** An echo of Jesus's words to the woman taken in adultery: 'Neither do I condemn thee' (John 8:11).

**line 745, '*Shemah Israel*':** These words, 'Hear, O Israel' (Deuteronomy 6:4), are the opening of one of Judaism's key prayers. The Shemah is recited twice daily, in the morning and the evening.

## Section XXII: 'The Church'

This section is strongly reminiscent of Section V of *The Waste Land*, 'What the Thunder Said', even to the extent of featuring some verbal parallels.

**line 751, 'dry sand beneath my boots':** Cf. Eliot's 'Sweat is dry and feet are in the sand' (*The Waste Land*, 337).

**line 755, 'care of Cook':** Thomas Cook (1808–92), the founder of the famous travel agency.

**lines 764–65, 'Sometimes one, sometimes the other / Led me by the arm':** Cf. Eliot's 'Who is the third who walks always beside you? / When I count, there are only you and I together / ... – But who is that on the other side of you?' (359–65).

**line 766, 'We stumbled across a harsh desert':** Cf. Eliot's 'Over endless plains, stumbling in cracked earth' (369).

**line 768, Anubis:** The Egyptian god of funerary rites, guide to the underworld. He was often depicted in art as a man with a dog's head.

**line 770, Sphynxes:** An alternative spelling of Sphinxes. A sphinx was a mythical creature with a human head and a lion's body; Greek sphinxes, which frequently also had wings, were female. Egyptian sphinxes were normally male. As representations of the Pharaoh's power, they often appeared in religious contexts. The most famous representation of a sphinx in Egyptian art is the Great Sphinx of Giza.

**lines 775–77, 'sounds of distant singing / Monotonous and poignant, / White-veiled women walked beside me':** Cf. Eliot's 'What is that sound high in the air / Murmur of maternal lamentation / Who are those hooded hordes swarming...' (366–69)

**lines 801–02, 'mitred god of porphyry... a curious rod':** Apparently a generic description of a statue of an ancient god rather than a reference to a specific deity. It bears some resemblance to the Egyptian Osiris, who wore a tall crown shaped like an elongated mitre and held a crook in one hand and a flail in the other. However, the Egyptians did not use porphyry for full-size statues.

**line 814, Lorenzo Valla** (*c.*1407–57): An Italian Renaissance humanist who proved that the Donation of Constantine (a supposed imperial decree transferring authority over Rome and the western empire and a great deal of imperial property to the Pope) was a forgery, thus attacking the presumption of the temporal power of the papacy.

The French footnote reads, 'A humanist, Lorenzo Valla (1467) demonstrated the falsehood of the Donation of Constantine, [and] of the correspondence of Jesus with Abgar of Edessa.' The church historian Eusebius (*c*.260–340 CE) mentions that the Edessan archives contained a correspondence between Abgar (d. *c*.50 CE) to Jesus, which modern scholars consider a forgery from (probably) the third century CE.

## Section XXIII: 'Quarrel with the Conjuror – The Dilemma Stated'

**line 844:** Virgil: See note on line 481.

**line 862:** The bust of Thomas Huxley, biologist and anthropologist (1825–95), is in the National Portrait Gallery.

## Section XXIV: 'Man's Insignificance – Youth and the Flame – Middle Age'

**line 891, 'O miserable condition of humanity':** Cf. Fulke Greville (1554–1628), 'O wearisome condition of humanity'; the opening line of the 'Chorus Sacerdotum' in *The Tragedy of Mustapha* (1609).

**line 893, 'princes and powers':** Cf. the New Testament injunction, 'Put them in mind to be subject to principalities and powers' (Titus 3:1; KJV).

**line 894, 'sweat and fardels bear':** Cf. Hamlet's lines in the 'To be or not to be' soliloquy: 'Who would fardels bear / To grunt and sweat under a weary life / but that the dread of something after death / The undiscovered country, from whose bourn / No traveller returns, puzzles the will…' (III.1.84–88). Cf. line 1331.

**lines 896–97, 'What's a man? / Fortuitous concurrence of whirling electrons':** Cf. *Hamlet*, 'What a piece of work is a man… this quintessence of dust' (II.2.327, 332).

**line 913, 'That way madness lies':** Cf. *King Lear*, 'O, that way madness lies' (III.4.24).

**lines 919–58:** These lines are the most directly autobiographical passage in the poem.

**line 919, 'So at twenty, I beheld the Gulf of Naples':** Aldington travelled in Italy with H.D. in the spring of 1913, when he was twenty. On the metres of this passage, see Introduction (p. 24).

**line 923, 'sirens... singing':** In the *Odyssey*, the Sirens are enchantresses who lure sailors to their deaths by the irresistible beauty of their singing. On Circe's advice, Odysseus plugs all his sailors' ears with wax so they cannot hear the Sirens, but has himself tied to the mast of the ship so that he can hear the Sirens' song without yielding to the desire to leap overboard and swim to them. This scene is common in ancient art, where the Sirens are often depicted as birds with women's heads.

**line 929, 'the daughters of the ocean':** The Oceanids, sea-nymphs, were daughters of the god Oceanus.

**line 933, 'fauns and dryads':** For fauns, see note on lines 710–11. Dryads were tree-nymphs. 'Faun' and 'Dryad' were Aldington's and H.D.'s most common pet names for one another.

**line 941, 'Whom the gods love dies in youth':** Proverbial; appears in Menander (*c*.342–290 BCE), fragment 4, and in Plautus (*c*.254–184 BCE), *Bacchides*, line 817. Herodotus illustrates the same idea in the story of Cleobis and Biton, who performed a great feat of piety when their mother needed to attend a festival of Hera. In the absence of oxen, the young men dragged an ox-cart carrying their mother to the hilltop temple five miles away. When their mother prayed to Hera for her sons to be granted whatever is best for human beings, Hera responded by causing the youths to die in their sleep (Herodotus I.31).

**lines 942–3, Death:** The personification of death as a female is not Greek; *thanatos* is a masculine word in Greek.

**line 948, 'Thrice Death clutched me':** This inverts the Homeric trope of a living man trying three times to embrace a ghost; cf. note on line 215. Aldington records in his memoir *Life for Life's Sake* that he had three close brushes with death during his military service, twice when he turned just as a shell whizzed past his head and once when his field glasses deflected a bullet (*Life for Life's Sake*, pp. 186–87).

**line 949, 'Then the gods abandoned me':** Cf. *The Waste Land*, line 175 and 179, 'The nymphs are departed.'

**line 958, 'Dante's *maggior dolore*':** Dante Alighieri (1265–1326), author of *The Divine Comedy*. Canto V of *The Inferno* tells the story of the adulterous lovers Paolo and Francesca, whom Dante meets in his journey through Hell. Francesca's '*Nessun maggior dolore / Che ricordarsi del tempo felice / Nella miseria*' ('There is no greater sorrow than to recall, in misery, a time of happiness') is one of the most famous quotations from the *Inferno*.

## *Section XXV: 'Impasse'*

**line 961, 'Most unbecoming men who strove with Kitchener':**
Field Marshal Herbert Kitchener (1850–1916) was instrumental in developing Britain's first mass army. Cf. Tennyson's 'Ulysses': 'Not unbecoming men that strove with gods' (line 53). In later reprintings of *Fool* Aldington changed this line to 'Most unbecoming men who strove with Haig', referring to Field Marshal Sir Douglas Haig (1861–1928), who took command of the British Expeditionary Force in 1915. The battles of the Somme and of Paschendaele took place under his direction. This change removes the feminine ending of 'men who strove with Kitchener', so that the revised line echoes Tennyson's line more closely in overall rhythm and in the monosyllabic ending. The change also shifts the focus from the Kitchener's Army volunteers of 1914 to the conscripted recruits who suffered such heavy losses under Haig.

**line 962, 'the bare bodkin':** An unsheathed dagger. Cf. Hamlet's '… when he himself might his quietus make / with a bare bodkin' (III.1.83–84). These words immediately precede the quotation at line 894.

**line 966, 'Plato or Aristotle, Zeno or Epicurus':** Plato: See note on line 372.

Aristotle: See note on line 686.

Zeno of Elea (fl. early fifth century BCE) is credited with four paradoxes involving motion. The most famous of these, often called the paradox of 'Achilles and the Tortoise', states that a faster runner can never catch a slower one because the distance between them can be infinitely subdivided.

Epicurus (341–270 BCE) held that the world consists of physical particles, the atoms (from Greek *atomos*, 'unable to be cut'). Even the soul consists of atoms and these, like the atoms composing the body, are dispersed at death; thus, there is no immortality of the soul. The gods exist, but are also composed of atoms, and take no interest in human affairs. Epicurus's moral philosophy taught that the ideal goal was *ataraxia*, lack of disturbance, which was to be achieved not by satisfying all desire for pleasure but by limiting the desires that one felt. Our knowledge of his teachings is heavily dependent on Lucretius's *De rerum natura* (first century BCE).

**line 968, 'a fine new chaos':** In the creation story told in Hesiod's *Theogony* (*c.*700 BCE), Chaos (Greek 'gap' or 'yawning') was the primordial entity that existed before Gaia (Earth).

**line 969–72, 'Phrygian shepherds... Ganymede':** Again, the speaker of the inset italicised lines is not identified. Aldington employs parody by giving a Greek twist to the familiar Christmas carol, 'While shepherds watched...'

Phrygia was an area of Asia Minor in west-central Anatolia (modern Turkiye). In Homer, the Phrygians were Trojan allies.

Ganymede was an exceptionally handsome adolescent Trojan prince from two generations before the Trojan War; he was the son of Priam's grandfather Tros. He was abducted by Zeus and made immortal, and served as the gods' cup-bearer.

**lines 977–79:** A reference to the 1915 rag-time song 'Are You from Dixie?', words by Jack Yellen and music by George L. Cobb.

**line 981:** John Philip Sousa (1854–1932), American composer of military marches.

**line 983:** A reference to the song 'Dance with a Dolly with a Hole in Her Stocking'. This song was first recorded in 1940, but versions of it were apparently known well before then.

**line 987, 'Old Sir Humpty-Dumpty':** Humpty-Dumpty is a character in a traditional nursery rhyme and appears in Lewis Carroll's *Through the Looking Glass* (1871). It is unclear if Aldington intends a reference to a specific artist here; if he does, the target may be Sir Francis Dicksee, who became President of the Royal Academy in 1924.

### *Section XXVI: 'War – Death of Mezzetin'*

**line 1007:** The Lewis gun was a First World War machine gun.

**line 1030, 'Mark VI':** This probably refers to a proposed British tank called the Mark VI, for which designs and mock-ups were produced in July 1917. The project was cancelled in December 1917 and the tank was never built. It could also refer to the Webley Revolver Mark VI, introduced in 1915, but this seems less likely in the context.

**line 1036, 'Bosch':** slang for a German soldier, normally spelt 'Boche'.

**line 1039, 'Verey lights... minnies':** Verey lights were flares of different colours, used in the First World War for signalling and lighting no man's land at night. They were fired from a pistol.

'Minnies' is an abbreviation of the German word 'Minnenwerfer', 'mine-thrower'. These were a kind of trench-mortar used from 1915 onwards. The word 'minnies' refers both to the mortar and to the bombs discharged from it.

**lines 1051–53, 'Who should remember you if we forget?...
dry-eyed and lousy':** No speaker is identified for these lines, but the
first-person plural of line 1051 argues against attributing them to 'I'.
It is tempting to read them as spoken, in effect, by Aldington himself;
cf. the address to the dead in his 1931 poem 'In Memory of Wilfred
Owen' (*The Complete Poems*, p. 302).

**line 1075, 'we'll make a man of you':** A reference to the last line
of Rudyard Kipling's poem 'If', 'you'll be a man, my son'.

**line 1081, 'as usual, my rifle was unloaded':** Aldington told his
friend Walter Lowenfels that he always carried his rifle unloaded at the
Front.

### Section XXVII: 'Mezzetin's Obituary'

**line 1094, 'Sir Hanley Podge':** We have been unable to identify any
original for this reference.

### Section XXVIII: 'Induction of Finale'

**line 1101, 'it flows on and on and on':** Cf. the sayings usually
attributed to Heraclitus, 'Everything flows' and 'one cannot step into the
same river twice'. On Heraclitus, see note on line 686.

### Section XXIX: 'Life in London with the Conjuror'

**line 1114, 'we'll make a man of you':** See note on line 1075.

**line 1141, 'a ticket for the British Museum':** The British Museum
Reading Room (now a separate institution, the British Library) required
prospective readers to apply for and receive a reader's ticket.

**lines 1149–50, 'the brisk discharge of volumes / From the forty
miles of magazine':** A reference to the British Museum's extensive
holdings in closed stacks and the system of retrieving books for readers.
The words 'discharge' and 'magazine' suggest military terminology.

### Section XXX: 'Hardships of the Rich'

**line 1156, 'Strong and cruel as an Assyrian king':** The British
Museum displays several bas-relief Assyrian sculptures, many of them
featuring kings engaged in activities such as reviewing captives and hunting.

**lines 1159–62:** The satirical target can be identified as Sir John Ellerman, reputed to be the richest man in England. Aldington recounts this conversation about coal with Sir John in *Life for Life's Sake* (pp. 193–94). Ellerman's daughter was the writer, Bryher, who became H.D.'s lifelong companion after H.D. and Aldington separated in 1919.

## Section XXXI: 'London by Night'

The narrator 'I' buries his imagination and intellectual qualities when he joins the depressing routine of lower-middle-class existence. Aldington reuses the material of the poem 'To Those who Played for Safety in Life' in *Exile* (p. 57). But he significantly moderates the harsh bitterness of another poem in *Exile*, 'Rhapsody in a Third-Class Carriage' (pp. 45–46). Aldington employs parataxis as he impressionistically lists the quotidian banalities of this dehumanised urban world, with the word 'There' at the beginning of fourteen lines. He recoils in horror at the thought of being condemned to follow the downbeat, repetitive routine of suburban existence.

**line 1176, 'Hydra-head':** The second of Heracles's Twelve Labours was to kill the Lernaean Hydra, a monstrous venomous snake with nine heads. When Heracles cut off one head, two more grew in its place. Heracles finally prevailed by having his nephew Iolaus cauterise the stump of each neck as he cut the head off, so that no new heads could grow. One head, however, was immortal; Heracles buried it under a massive boulder.

**line 1177, 'Anarchist attacks':** In the late nineteenth and early twentieth centuries, there were repeated terrorist attacks by anarchists in Britain, Europe and the United States. These included bombings in which innocent bystanders were killed and injured.

**lines 1222–23, 'Time is patient... within her bosom':** Again, Aldington changes the gender from the classical personification, where Time is masculine.

## Section XXXII: 'I Murder the Conjuror'

**line 1240:** Captain James Cook (1728–79), British explorer, cartographer and naval officer.

**line 1241–42, 'Dead dogs drifting out to sea / And Nashe's Isle of Dogs:** Thomas Nashe (1567–1601), satirist, pamphleteer and playwright. With Ben Jonson he co-wrote the play *The Isle of Dogs* which was immediately suppressed; no known copy exists. The Isle of Dogs is now the location of the Canary Wharf office complex. Cf. *The Waste Land*, 'The barges wash / Drifting logs / Down Greenwich reach / Past the Isle of Dogs' (273–76).

**line 1243, 'and patata and patati':** *Et patati et patata* is a French expression meaning 'and so on and so forth'.

**lines 1261–64:** Aldington's target is unmistakeably Kipling, with references to his 'ifs' and the line 'We'll make a man of you, my son'; cf. lines 1071 and 1110. If Kiplingesque attitudes are despised, by contrast, Byron's name is honoured (Section IV).

**line 1272, 'Roman coins':** The bed of the Thames contained (and still contains) coins, pottery shards and other relics of Roman Londinium.

## Section XXXIII: 'The Good Citizen'

This section lists the depressing features of the character's life of frustrated ambition and lofty hopes. It can be read as an ironic commentary on lines 61–65 in Section I of *The Waste Land*, 'The Burial of the Dead' (see also Introduction, p. 26). Aldington's 'I', now a suburban commuter and an 'Empire-Builder and Tax-Payer', reflects the crowd of 'dead' who 'flow' over Eliot's London Bridge.

**line 1314, 'Tell myself that I've been made a Man':** Ironically, 'I' does not seem to recognise the echo of Kipling and of the Conjuror here.

**lines 1318–19, 'Scraps of song and distant laughter / Tinkling of a ghostly mandoline':** Cf. *The Waste Land*, lines 259–65.

**line 1321, 'Of a life once vowed to truth and beauty':** Cf. the closing lines of Keats's 'Ode on a Grecian Urn'; '"Beauty is truth, truth beauty" – that is all / Ye know on earth, and all ye need to know'.

## Section XXXIV: 'Valediction'

No speaker is specified for this final italicised section.

**line 1330, 'lament for the birth of a babe':** Cf. Sophocles, *Oedipus at Colonus* ll. 1224–25: 'Not to be born is best of all'.

**line 1331, 'to the bourn':** An echo of Hamlet's 'the undiscovered country from whose bourn / No traveller returns' (III.1.87–88). Cf. line 894.

# Works Cited

Aldington, Richard, *Exile and Other Poems*, ed. Elizabeth Vandiver and Vivien Whelpton (London: Renard Press, 2023)

Aldington, Richard, *A Book of 'Characters' from Theophrastus; Joseph Hall, Sir Thomas Overbury ... and Other English Authors; Jean de la Bruyere, Vavenargues, and Other French Authors.* (London: Routledge; New York: Dutton, 1924)

Aldington, Richard, *Voltaire* (London: George Routledge; New York, E. P. Dutton, 1925)

Aldington, Richard (trans.), *Fifty Romance Lyric Poems* (New York: Crosby Gaige, 1928)

Aldington, Richard, *The Poems* (Garden City, NY: Doubleday, Doran, 1934)

Aldington, Richard, *Life for Life's Sake: A Book of Reminiscences* (New York: Viking, 1941)

Aldington, Richard, *The Complete Poems* (London: Allan Wingate, 1948)

Gates, Norman T. (ed.), *The Poetry of Richard Aldington: A Critical Evaluation and An Anthology of Uncollected Poems* (University Park, PA, and London: Pennsylvania University Press, 1974)

## ALSO AVAILABLE BY RICHARD ALDINGTON
## FROM RENARD PRESS

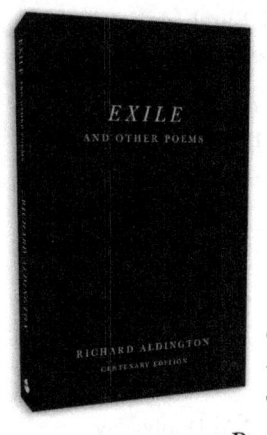

First published in 1923, *Exile and Other Poems* is an important, poignant collection from one of the foremost Imagist war poets. Penned after witnessing the horrors of the frontline during the First World War, Aldington's brutal, honest verse lays bare unimaginable experiences.

The first part of the collection, 'Exile', explores the poet's survivor's guilt, post-traumatic stress and sense of alienation. The collection continues with a 'Songs for Puritans' and 'Songs for Sensualists', pastiches of seventeenth and eighteenth-century love poetry, and a series of more personal poems exploring the natural world, from which Aldington drew reassurance.

Enriched with a fascinating introduction and explanatory notes by leading Aldington scholars Elizabeth Vandiver and Vivien Whelpton, this centenary edition seeks to place Exile firmly back on the map of war poetry, from which it has been missing for too long.

'This new edition, beautifully produced by Renard
for Aldington's centenary, would be worth having just for the
first-rate introduction and the detailed background notes which
give a very clear summmary of his troubles.'
John Greening, *PN Review*

ISBN: 9781804470701
Paperback • £10 • 100pp